Journal of a
Teenage Genius

HELEN V. GRIFFITH

Journal of a Teenage Genius

HARCOURT BRACE & COMPANY

Orlando   Atlanta   Austin   Boston   San Francisco   Chicago   Dallas   New York
Toronto   London

This edition is published by special arrangement
with Greenwillow Books, a division of William
Morrow & Company, Inc.

Grateful acknowledgment is made to
Greenwillow Books, a division of William
Morrow & Company, Inc. for permission to
reprint *Journal of a Teenage Genius* by Helen
V. Griffith, cover illustration by Frank Modell.
Copyright © 1987 by Helen V. Griffith.
Printed in the United States of America

ISBN 0-15-305233-3

1 2 3 4 5 6 7 8 9 10   060   97 96 95 94

For my mother

Saturday, August 20

9:00 A.M.

Success at last! I have achieved what nobody outside of a science-fiction novel has ever done! My place in history is secure.

In another fifteen minutes the liquid bubbling in a beaker over my Bunsen burner should reach sufficient heat for the necessary chemical change to occur, and I will have invented the formula for the transmutation of matter!

Since the dawn of science, men have attempted to discover this secret, but it took me, a young, unknown genius, to finally come up with a formula that will change one kind of metal into another. Iron into gold! Tin into silver! Wow! Mind-boggling, isn't it?

I feel that I should write my impressions of this great moment, because naturally the scientific world will be agog with curiosity about me and my work once my discovery comes to light.

First, some background. It's been a long, lonely road, and being a genius really isn't as great as you might think, mainly because nobody else takes you seriously. My mother, for instance. My mother, *especially*. She keeps saying that I don't understand what I'm doing, that it's dangerous, that I should perform my experiments in school with supervision. In other words, she talks as if I'm just an ordinary kid playing with a chemistry set.

I am working under very difficult conditions in our unequipped, poorly lit garage because my own mother has turned me out of our own basement, just because of a few minor mishaps that could happen to any scientist.

Such as the odor from one of my earlier experiments forcing us all to leave the house for the weekend. But did I complain? Even though it set me back in my work, I put up with the inconvenience and relaxed and enjoyed swimming in the motel pool.

My parents weren't such good sports, though. My mother even claimed the smell made Toodles sick. As if anything could get Toodles down. My mother worries over him as if he were a baby, and he's just a hyperactive little poodle. I think we probably would have stayed home that weekend, smell and all, if it hadn't been for Toodles.

The latest incident is the one that drove me from my basement lab, and the whole thing was Toodles's fault. He was watching me work, like the nosy little mutt he is, and just as I picked up a test tube of one of my chemical solutions, he jumped up on my leg to get a better look and I spilled the stuff right in his face.

You never heard such yelping in your life. And you never saw the mother of a teenage boy move so fast. She was down those basement stairs in about two leaps, sized up the situation in an instant, and, brushing aside my reassurances that the chemical—although irritating—was not dangerous, she stuck Toodles in the sink and turned the water on him.

After she washed him off he quit yelping and just

stood there shivering and looking about half his size. I would have welcomed a quiet discussion of my mother's misunderstanding of the danger involved, but she kept saying things like, "That does it" and "This can't go on" and "That kid," so it seemed wise to defer any more explanations and to move my equipment before she did something that we would both regret.

When my journal is made public, she'll realize how wrong she was, and though I'm sorry the world has to know of her lack of foresight, still this is a factual account of the greatest scientific breakthrough of the age, and it may be an encouragement to other geniuses not to give up just because their mothers don't have faith in them or appreciate their abilities.

At this moment the solution in the beaker is bubbling away like crazy. I must record this while it is happening. It's turning wild colors and boiling and steaming and—oh, wow—it almost looks like it's going to . . .

SAME DAY, 10:00 A.M.

It did. And I'm in big trouble.

I'm writing this in my room where I have come to escape a mother's wrath. She keeps saying, "You could have been injured, maybe even killed," and she's not even concerned that the greatest scientific discovery of the age just blew up.

There wasn't really that much damage, anyway. I

mean, what's a broken window? The real disaster is that I failed. And my notebook with all my calculations in it is gone, destroyed in the explosion.

The work of years is now a puddle on the garage floor, and it doesn't take a genius to know that my experimenting days are over, at least around here. My father will be less than joyful when he sees the garage, and my mother is overreacting, as usual.

She must be calming down somewhat, though, because I can hear her calling her precious Toodles. If anything can cheer her up, he will.

And so, fellow scientists, I shall take this opportunity to return to the garage and see what I can salvage.

SAME DAY, 11:00 A.M.

Scientists of the world, what I have to report now is going to set you all on your ears.

As I slipped into the garage I almost stumbled over a little curly-haired boy about five or six years old who was sitting all huddled up on the floor, wearing a bewildered expression and nothing else.

"Who are you?" I asked. "Are you lost or something?"

The little boy's lips started to quiver and he said, "I'm Toodles."

Being a genius, a horrible suspicion of the truth dawned on me instantly, but I said skeptically, "What do you mean, you're Toodles?" and right away the little boy started to cry out loud, and between sobs he said, "I *am* Toodles, only there's something wrong with me. I came in to look around and I found a nice puddle on the floor and I lapped it up and then I felt funny and all at once my fur was gone and I'm cold. And my nose is dry."

Well, you can imagine my amazement, not to mention my consternation, because my experiments in the transmutation of matter were not for the purpose of turning little dogs into little boys, but evidently that is just what has happened.

Some words of my mother's about danger and fooling with things I don't understand sneaked into my brain, but I pushed them out again. How could it be wrong to try to advance scientific knowledge?

Looking at Toodles, though, crying tears all over the garage floor, I saw that there was more to science than cold facts. I hadn't given any thought to what effects my experiment might have. I'd had no idea it would work on living creatures. And if there was a way to reverse the process, I hadn't discovered it yet.

And now my normally nimble brain seems to be clogged with molasses. I can't really grasp what has happened, much less predict the consequences.

All I've done so far is sneak Toodles into my room and dress him in some old stuff of mine. Everything is too big, but that can't be helped. Nobody noticed he wasn't wearing clothes when he was a furry little dog, but now it's obvious to the most casual observer.

At this moment Mom is combing the neighborhood for the dog-Toodles, while the boy-Toodles is here being his usual busybody self, only on two legs instead of four. He's having a great time going through my bureau drawers, something he wasn't able to do when he had only paws, and he seems contented enough at the moment, at least. But what am I going to do with him? How will I explain him? Without the formula to prove my story no one will believe the truth, I know that. They'll probably think I'm a kidnapper. I can see it now—like those old movies on TV—me, in a hard chair in the middle of a bare room, bright lights blinding me, harsh voices saying over and over, "Okay, talk. Where did you get the kid?" and me saying, "He's my mother's poodle."

As you can see, the situation is impossible. Not to mention that I seem to be losing my grip. I must not panic. There has to be a sane, reasonable way out of this mess.

Poor Mom. I can hear her in the yard now, calling Toodles. I know she's worr—

SAME DAY, 12:00 NOON

That was close. When Toodles heard my mother's voice, he took off down the hall like a shot, but I grabbed him and dragged him back here and we came to an understanding. I hope.

I told him that for the time being his name is Tommy, he's new in the neighborhood, and he's a *boy*. I guess he understands what I mean. He just said, "Okay," and then curled up in a ball on the floor and sighed.

My mother is calling me for lunch. This is the moment of truth. Will Toodles act the way I told him, or will he drink out of his bowl on the floor? Will Mom recognize Toodles in human form? Will she notice that the clothes he's wearing are mine? And will I break out into the hysterical laughter I feel coming on?

If this is the last notation in my journal, you can draw your own conclusions.

SAME DAY, 1:00 P.M.

Fellow scientists, Toodles cannot be depended on. He is not a boy, he is a two-footed poodle.

As soon as we entered the kitchen, he ran to my mother, wrapped his arms around her knees, and looked up at her adoringly with his big brown eyes.

"Why, who is this?" said my mother. "What a cute little boy."

I told her my prearranged story and felt like a rat for lying, although it wasn't totally a lie, he *was* a new kid in town. Then Mom told me about Toodles being gone and how worried she was and I felt like a *double* rat.

We got through lunch somehow, but it was touch and go, especially as Tommy showed a tendency to lap his soup and afterward asked for a biscuit. Fortunately my mother thought he meant a cookie.

After he ate his cookie he sat on the floor by my mother's chair and put his chin on her knee. With those brown eyes and that mop of curly hair he looked so much like the original Toodles that I didn't see how my mother could help but notice.

She didn't, though. She just looked kind of surprised and said, "Such a friendly child. Do you go to school, Tommy?"

Toodles said, "No, but I'm smart. I can sit up, roll over, and shake hands."

Before he could demonstrate, I grabbed him by the wrist and pulled him out of the room after me, muttering something about reading him a story.

And now here I am back in my room trying to calm Toodles, who is whimpering that he is cold and that everything feels wrong.

Poor Toodles. I've really messed up his life, not to mention how bad my mother feels without her little dog. I'm beginning to think I never should have tried such a risky experiment by myself. I should have anticipated the possibility of something going wrong and been prepared for it. I should have listened to my mo—no, I won't go that far.

Enough of these recriminations. Away with this self-pity. Am I a genius or a clod? I have things to do. I have to set up a new lab somewhere. And I need a place to hide Toodles while I work on an antidote. In the meantime he stays locked in my room. I'm afraid of what he might do if he saw a cat.

SAME DAY, 2:00 P.M.

Joy and euphoria! My mother is mad at me, my scientific career is at an end, my whole experiment was a flop, but I don't care. And do you know why I don't care, scientists of the world? Because Toodles is Toodles again! Yes, little curly-haired Tommy is now little curly-haired Toodles, and I've never seen a happier dog.

I was standing in the garage waiting for an inspiration when my mother came storming in wanting to know what kind of game I was playing. It seems she heard whining and scratching at my bedroom door, and when she opened it, there was Toodles, all tangled up in some old clothes. She thinks I was hiding him from her as some kind of a mixed-up joke.

I'll square things with her later, but for now I just want to sit here in my old garage-lab and appreciate my narrow escape.

Apparently the emulsion wasn't stable. The experiment was an even worse failure than I thought at first. What luck! I feel as if I've been given a second chance at life. I don't have to be a scientist. I'll be a wrestler or a cowboy. I'll be sensible. I'll throw all my scientific equipment away and sit around watching TV like everybody else.

Little Toodles just came bouncing into the garage in high spirits. I wonder if he remembers anything about his adventure. He doesn't act like it. He's playing with something he found outside, throwing it into the air and pouncing on it when it lands. Hey, wait a minute—

SAME DAY, 2:20 P.M.

Fellow scientists, take heart. All is not lost. What Toodles was playing with was my *notebook* with the *formula* in it. It must have been blown out of the garage window in the explosion. For once busybodiness has paid off.

I can't wait to get to work. I'll set up a secret laboratory. I'll work day and night. I'll—what am I saying? Haven't I learned anything from today's experiences?

The answer to that question is—you bet I have!

I'll cool it for a while. I'll study. I'll plan. I'll listen to other scientists and try (despite my convictions to the contrary) to stop thinking I know it all.

I'll still be a genius, but I'll be a *smart* genius.

Wednesday, August 31

Fellow scientists, genius cannot be suppressed. I really intended to wait until I had a more solid scientific education, but inventing is in my blood. Besides, is it right to make the world wait for whatever it is my fertile brain comes up with next?

I'm reinstating myself very slowly so as not to alarm my parents, who are oddly unsupportive of my efforts.

At this moment I am in my newly set up lab in the basement, surrounded by all the paraphernalia necessary for my work, at least all I can afford. I even have a cage of white mice waiting to do their part for science. I'm not sure yet what that will be, but they add a nice touch.

Those mice are the only reason I was able to move from the garage back to the basement. My mother the animal lover decided they would be cold in the garage.

They must be contented. They recently donated three more subjects to the lab—Huey, Dewey, and Louie. I know they're duck names, fellow scientists. Don't hold me responsible. My mother named them. I've gone along with her on that, but the parents' names are coolly scientific—Mouse M (the male) and Mouse F (the female).

I've tried to explain to my mother the difference between laboratory animals and pets, but she can't grasp the distinction. She just says, "Don't you hurt Huey, Dewey, or Louie. Or Mickey or Minnie, either." That's what she calls the parents. At least they're mouse names.

Toodles is even more interested in the mice than my mother is. He examines the cage every day—for weaknesses, no doubt—and then tries to snuff the mice through the wire. His various close calls haven't prejudiced him against science. He spends all his spare moments frisking around the lab, and Toodles has a lot of spare moments. It's not conducive to scientific thought to have a furry muzzle rooting through your papers or little teeth hanging on to your pant leg. I'll bet Einstein's mother didn't have a dog.

Just now I'm trying to formulate a suitable project to devote myself to—something that will lighten mankind's burdens, advance civilization, make me rich and famous. Only joking. I don't need to be rich.

What I need is something worth my involvement, something that will be a real contribution to science. I won't write in this journal again until I can record the great humanitarian work I intend to pursue.

Wednesday, September 7

I have made my decision. My next invention will be something to make me grow three inches taller.

Wait, fellow scientists. Don't throw this journal down in disgust. I know my project seems selfish, even frivolous. But I didn't make the decision lightly. And I'm sure the discovery will have numerous applications once it is developed and made public. I'll think of something.

The fact is, scientists of the world, I'm in love.

I can see you all now, sitting openmouthed in amazement after reading that last sentence. But why should it be so amazing? Granted I'm a genius, but in all other ways I'm a normal (though far from average) teenage man.

Fellow scientists, have you ever been in love? I don't mean like Romeo and Juliet or David and Bathsheba. I mean, *really* in love. It was today in Chemistry class, across a crowded lab table, that I first glimpsed Loretta Bringhurst. We were all doing our first experiment of the school year. Most of the class doesn't know a Bunsen burner from a charcoal grill. It's pathetic to watch them. It's also pathetic to think I have to work side by side with these numskulls for the rest of the year.

I was halfheartedly setting up my materials, preparing to begin the extremely rudimentary experiment assigned to us, when I happened to notice Loretta. She was already well into the task. She didn't check the book for each step the way the rest of the kids were doing. She knew what to do. She mixed chemicals with a confidence, a fearlessness, an authority that filled me with awe. I just stood and gazed.

When I came back to earth, it was too late for me to do my own experiment, and Mr. Lambert made it clear that I would receive a zero for the day. Not a very auspicious start to the school year, but then it's not every day you fall in love. At least it's not every day *I* fall in love. Girls have not loomed large in my life heretofore.

How can I describe Loretta so that you will see her as I do? The first word that comes to mind is *tall*. Actually she's not all that tall. And I'm not all that short. But she's taller than I am. You'd think my stature in the scientific community would render me impervious to feelings of inadequacy about my height, but when I am in the company of a girl who is taller than me, I feel like a kid. What's worse, I begin to act like one.

Let me illustrate. After class I approached Loretta purposefully, intending to congratulate her on her ability to turn a boring experiment into a showstopper.

"Loretta," I began.

She turned and just stood there being taller than me. Immediately I reverted to half my age.

"Um," I said. "Ah."

She looked impatient. I was desperate.

"Uh, you're new here, aren't you?" I asked feebly. Even my voice sounded half its age.

Loretta nodded and waited, but I had said all I was capable of uttering. She turned away and I had to let her go.

So you see, fellow scientists, I have to be taller. If I were willing to wait a year or two, nature would probably take care of the problem. But I can't afford to wait. While I stand around growing, she might become involved with some clod who would just be attracted by her looks or her personality instead of her remarkable scientific ability. He might encourage her to waste her time at dances or football games or riding around in cars with the radio on loud.

I can't let that happen. She belongs here in the lab helping me discover the secrets of the universe. But as long as there is a discrepancy in our heights, our relationship will remain static.

And so I've decided to give nature a little assistance. As it happens, I've done some previous work in growth encouraging. It came about when I ran over my mother's favorite rosebush with the lawn mower and was hoping to restore it before she noticed. She noticed, so I never finished, but I have all the preliminary research somewhere around here.

Two or three inches should do it. I don't have to tower over her.

Friday, September 9

A quick entry to report that I found my notes on my Growth Encourager. They look good. My usual careful work and patient recording of results will make the rest of my work a piece of cake.

Toodles, who considers himself my research assistant, examined the papers briefly in his doggy way, but aside from some wrinkles and slobber, they seem to be all right. What did I do to deserve this dog?

Friday, September 16

9:00 P.M.

Work proceeding normally. I have prepared some Growth Encourager using my old research as a guideline. I had to make some critical changes, of course, since I'm now dealing with animals instead of plants, but I'm able to conquer such difficulties because that's just the way I am. Not to brag.

I'm having a serious problem with Toodles. He loves the smell of my Growth Encourager almost as much as he loves the smell of mice. I try to sneak down here when he's not watching, but as soon as he misses me, he scratches at the basement door and whines. I could stand the whining, but my mother can't stand the scratches in the paint, so as usual, Toodles gets his way. If this were Growth Reverser instead of Growth Encourager, I might be tempted to give him a big swig. Forgive me, fellow scientists. That was an unworthy thought. He's really a cute little dog with a puppy's natural curiosity. You should see him now, looking up at the mice cage with his head cocked to one side and his little pink tongue sticking out and agggh—

SAME DAY, 10:00 P.M.

Scientists of the world, Toodles attacked the mice—an unprovoked attack on five innocent caged creatures. He bounced like a rubber ball from floor to stool to table to cage in the time it took me to say, "Agggh." Fellow scientists, we are talking here about a dog that is so helpless, he has to be carried over puddles in the street.

He knocked the cage off the table and the mice went in five different directions. So did Toodles, it seemed, until I grabbed him by the scruff of his neck, carried him upstairs, and slammed the door on him. I can hear him snuffling up there, but he's afraid to scratch. He knows he went too far this time.

I caught the three babies right away, and after about a half hour of stalking, I came up with control Mouse F, but Mouse M, my potential subject, is lying low. Maybe tomorrow he'll be hungry enough or lonely enough to come back, but I seriously doubt it. If he has any sense at all, he'll move to a house without a poodle.

Saturday, September 17

Mouse M has not returned. I've decided to do the experiment with Huey instead. Or Dewey or Louie. It doesn't matter. I don't like to experiment on Mouse F in case she is expecting another litter. You never know about mice.

Huey, Dewey, and Louie are identical. White fur and red eyes, your typical laboratory mouse. I've put an ink dot on the back of each one—red for Huey, blue for Dewey, green for Louie.

As soon as I complete this entry, I will fill an eye-dropper with Growth Encourager and Huey will have a before-bedtime drink. Then, if all goes well—and why shouldn't it?—it won't be long before Huey is no longer identical to Dewey and Louie.

Since I'm not sure of the exact dosage necessary to trigger the growth mechanism, I plan to start with a small dose and gradually increase the amount until a reaction results.

Tuesday, September 20

    I'm having a slight, unanticipated problem. Huey hates the Growth Encourager. For his first dose I held him in one hand with my fingers around his head so I could turn him on his back and squirt the solution into his mouth. He didn't resist until he got a taste of the stuff and then he went crazy. I dumped him back in the cage, and he sat there rubbing his mouth with his paws and sticking out his tongue. I never thought a mouse could register revulsion.

    The second night he tried to hide, and the third night he bit me. Not hard, but he meant it. From now on I'm wearing gloves when handling that little rodent.

Thursday, September 22

A brief entry, fellow world changers, to report nothing happening so far. However, I am confident of results in a few days. You can't rush scientific discovery.

Friday, September 23

4:30 P.M.

Fellow scientists, scientific discovery is going to have to be rushed. Before Chem lab I saw my fears realized when Loretta was accosted in the hall by our resident rock singer, Maynard Manning, better known in this school as Main Man. His specialty is shouting unintelligible songs at the audience while waving a large guitar. Nobody knows if he can play it or not, but it doesn't seem to matter.

He and Loretta had a short but serious talk, during which the urge was strong in me to leap at him with a scream and a karate kick. Since I don't know karate, I resisted the urge.

I pulled a second zero in Chem lab as I observed another brilliant performance by Loretta. What artistry! What grace! It was like watching a chemical ballet. When she finished and held up the test tube to see the results, it was all I could do to keep from shouting, "Bravo!" I knew then that I could wait no longer. I have to make my move before that song shouter ruins her career and my life.

When class was over, I hurried to her.

"Loretta," I said.

She turned and waited.

"Uh, I hope you like it here," I squeaked.

"Thanks," she said to the kid I had just become.

She walked away. Main Man was waiting for her at the door.

As soon as I got home I checked the mouse. No change. And now I'm going to take a short break to give way to utter despair.

SAME DAY, 4:40 P.M.

I'm back. And not only did I not give way, I decided to call Loretta. Why didn't I think of this before? On the phone I can't see the difference in our heights. My true personality will come through. After a few conversations she'll be crazy about me. Then it will just be a case of love by telephone until I grow or until Huey does.

SAME DAY, 6:30 P.M.

I called, and the timetable on my Growth Encourager will have to be speeded up. I'm still not sure how it all happened. I dialed the phone and sat there taking deep breaths so my voice wouldn't shake. Finally someone answered and I said, "Hi, is Loretta there?"

"No, this is her mother," the voice said. "Who is this and what do you want and give me all the details of your life from the age of three."

Well, that's not really what she said, but it felt that way. She was bursting with questions. She even asked me if I played the guitar and sounded disappointed when I said no. I could have told her that as a genius I could probably pick it up in an hour or two, but being modest I didn't mention my IQ and numerous scientific triumphs. Well, near triumphs. It amused me to let her think she was speaking to just an average teenager, which we all know is far from the fact. Anyway, she kept me on the phone for about twenty minutes, and when we hung up, I had a date with Loretta. For tonight.

I've never made a date with a girl through her mother before. Let's be honest, I've never made a date with a girl, period. I've been too busy securing my place in the annals of greatness. But just because I'm inexperienced doesn't mean I don't know anything, and I'm pretty sure this isn't how it's done.

The Bringhursts live only three blocks away, which is fortunate, since I'm not old enough to drive. When Mrs. Bringhurst described the house, I recognized it easily. It's one of the oldest houses in the neighborhood and it's where Maynard Manning lived until a few months ago.

I'm to pick Loretta up at eight and take her to a rock concert in the park. It's not the activity I would have chosen for our first date, especially since Main Man is the main attraction. The concert was her mother's idea. I couldn't protest. Loretta's mother was overwhelming over the phone. I shudder to think what she'll be like in person.

At the supper table I told my parents about my

date. They didn't seem as surprised about it as I was. In fact, they look at it as a natural occurrence.

My mother wanted to know about Loretta's family, but since I didn't know, I couldn't say. My father looked as if he might speak, but I didn't give him an opening. I was afraid he wanted to follow up on the stork-is-a-myth talk he gave me some years ago.

As it happened, he didn't tell me any too soon. I had been working on a birth control plan that involved scaring the storks away before they could land—something on the order of the loud noises they use to break up large populations of blackbirds. Think of the time I could have wasted. It was hard to accept the fact that all that work was meaningless, but it did make me understand why nobody had ever thought of it before. I'd wondered about that. I would advise other geniuses not to get into the area of family planning at least until you can read. There's too much they don't tell you.

It's getting closer and closer to date time, and I'm getting more and more nervous. I shouldn't have made this date. I shouldn't have let Loretta's mother railroad me into this. I'm not ready. I'm still short. I'll act like somebody's baby brother all evening instead of like the worldly, sophisticated genius I actually am. Then she'll never take another chance on me. She'll go off with that guitar brandisher and forget all about the true happiness that only science can bring.

In another few weeks something is bound to happen with my Growth Encourager. Why didn't I wait? I let a little competition panic me. Once I was taller, I could have cut out Main Man easily.

Sorry, fellow scientists, sometimes I forget this is a scientific journal. It's facts you want, not feelings. But it's a fact that I'm feeling miserable.

Should I cancel my date? No, I can't do it. Maybe I could hire a cab and get the driver to cruise us around all evening. If I didn't stand up, I wouldn't know I was shorter and I could be my everyday fascinating self. You're right, it's a ridiculous idea. But I'm finding it hard to concentrate what with this fast-approaching date and the fact that I hear footsteps running up and down the basement stairs, and some of them are dog footsteps. I can't stand it. I have to investigate.

SAME DAY, 7:00 P.M.

Scientists of the world, the mouse has grown! I can hardly believe it. Why do I say that? Of course I can believe it. It's what I've been working toward, isn't it?

What a beautiful sight. There are Dewey and Louie with their blue and green spots, respectively, busily shredding newspaper, their favorite pastime. There is Mouse F. Her favorite pastime is shredding newspaper, too, now that Mouse M has flown the coop. And there is Huey, as big as his mother, with no apparent ill effects from his transformation. He's gorging on oatmeal flakes right now. He's lost his red ink spot, but otherwise he's fine. He doesn't even act scared of me anymore. Being larger must have given him courage.

I don't know what was going on, but by the time I got downstairs, there was nobody here but mice. I should have been here when Huey grew, instead of holed up in my room trying to fit heel lifts into my sneakers and (you might as well know all) blow-drying my hair straight up to give it height.

When I see what I've achieved, I really ask myself why I feel I have to impress Loretta. *I'm* the genius. She should feel that she has to impress *me*.

But I'm a realist, fellow scientists. And for that reason I did some quick computations, considering the difference in size between Huey and me, and the length of time it took him to grow, and the time it will take me to get to Loretta's, and came up with the amount of Growth Encourager I should take to be tall for tonight.

I know, I know, fellow scientists. This isn't the way it's done. But a truly innovative scientist has to dare to take risks. He or she has to put his or her theories to the test before he or she can realize his or her dreams and reach his or her—oh, forget it.

SAME DAY, 7:15 P.M.

Fellow scientists, Huey is absolutely right. This stuff is revolting. I made so many grimaces and groans trying to get it down that Toodles came running to investigate. He watched me with his ears straight up for a minute and then backed away and ran upstairs, yelping. But it's swallowed. It's beginning its growth-encouraging work. At least, I hope it is. I don't feel anything but this disgusting taste in my mouth.

I'm preparing to leave for Loretta's. No doubt my next entry will record the brilliant success of my growth-encouraging work.

SAME DAY, 7:45 P.M.

Something has just occurred, fellow scientists, that causes me great uneasiness of mind. I'm sitting on the curb near Loretta's house, hoping I'll do some last-minute growing, but to tell you the truth, I think my experiment has—well, I won't say *failed*. Let's just say that the results are as yet not evident.

I waited as long as I could, hoping something would happen before I left for Loretta's, but nothing seemed to be going on—at least not outwardly. A glance at my extensive calculations provided no clues, but there wasn't time for an in-depth study. It was time to pick up Loretta. Something more elemental than the thirst for knowledge was driving me to her. I had to go, even if I spent the evening putting crickets down her back.

I had hoped my parents would let me go without comment, but no such luck.

"What did you do to your hair?" my mother asked, and my father said, "Is that how you dress for a date?"

My mother said, "That's how *you* dressed," and my

father said, "I'd hoped for better things from the next generation."

It wasn't a conversation I felt I could contribute anything meaningful to, so I said, "See you later."

Reminded of my presence, they both ordered me to have fun. I could see my father resisting the urge to tell me to what extent.

My mother walked me outside, and Toodles nosed his way out the door with us.

"You little detective," my mother said affectionately. She grabbed him up and kissed him while he wiggled like a lizard.

"He found Mickey, did you notice?" she asked me.

I had to stop and think who Mickey was. His professional name, as you know, is Mouse M.

"He brought him to me in his little mouth without harming him a bit," she continued proudly.

Since it was Toodles who let the mouse out in the first place, I didn't think he rated a medal for retrieving him, but the fact is, fellow scientists, when it comes to Toodles, my mother's logic is not logical. I told her I'd check the mouse when I got home and left her standing there congratulating Toodles. I headed for Loretta's house, running tall.

About halfway there my mother's words rang a little bell in my head. Toodles had found Mickey, she said. Mickey is Mouse M—the father mouse. The bell in my head became a gong. The louder it rang, the slower I ran, until I was just standing on the sidewalk, staring into space. At least that was how it would appear to any passerby. Actually I was facing reality.

You can see it already, can't you, fellow scientists? Your well-developed deductive powers make a detailed explanation unnecessary. It is now obvious to us all that what I took to be a large Huey was just a normal-sized Mouse M, recaptured by Toodles the hero and returned to his cage by my mother. That explains all that running up and down the stairs while I was trying to give myself tall hair.

Why didn't I give more thought to the fact that the mouse I was calling a grown-up Huey had no red spot on its back? Because I wanted the mouse to be Huey—that's why. Believe me, you can't be thinking any worse of me than I am. I have been guilty of gross negligence, stupid carelessness, monumental conceit.

Look at it this way, fellow scientists. It takes a big man to make big mistakes.

So tonight is shot. If Huey didn't grow, I won't, either. I'm doomed to spend a whole evening with Loretta while I'm still short—which means I'll revert to kindergarten humor and ruin my chances with her forevermore.

Well, it can't be helped. I have to go through with it. At least if she's with me, she's not with Maynard Manning.

My uneasiness of mind is caused by this nagging question: Where is Huey?

SAME DAY, 9:00 P.M.

This entry is being written to the beat of "Tiger Woman on the Beach," written and performed by the Rock Chompers from my own high school. They wanted a name that sounded tough and bad, but Rock Chompers makes people laugh. That's just as well, because you have to be in a good mood to tolerate their music at all.

I'm not in a good mood, fellow scientists, but something is happening that demands my total concentration, and a whole beach full of tiger women couldn't divert me.

I'm sitting on a grassy hillside under a starry sky sharing soft drinks and pretzels with Loretta, and you'd think I would feel on top of the world. I don't. Even the noise being produced by the Rock Chompers in the name of entertainment, which has mesmerized the rest of the audience, fails to reach me. While they sit, their brains beaten into submission by several glittering guitars and a large, complicated set of drums, I am writing furiously in my journal.

It has to be done, fellow scientists, even though it's crowded and noisy and Loretta is watching me with an expression I can't read.

At the risk of sounding overly dramatic, I will note that this evening's experiences must be recorded while there is *still time*. There are reasons, which I am about to relate, why this may be the last entry in the journal you are now eagerly devouring. And if my writing becomes very tiny and gradually vanishes altogether, you'll know that my worst fears have been realized.

I arrived at Loretta's a different person from the carefree boy who left my house a few minutes earlier. Well, I hadn't been exactly carefree before, but in comparison.

I rang the bell, hoping her mother would answer to kind of get us over any initial shyness, but Loretta opened the door. I swallowed. She waited.

"Hi, I'm Zack Longwood," I said finally.

"I know," she said.

Several hours seemed to go by.

"I'm sorry I'm late," I said. Actually I wasn't late, but I couldn't think of anything else to say.

"Late for what?" Loretta asked.

I tried to look behind her into the house. Where was her mother? I was beginning to suspect this date was a secret between her and me.

"I was under the impression," I began. "I was told—"

"Have you been talking to my mother?" Loretta asked.

"Well, you weren't home," I said, sounding like a guilty kid. "She said you'd like to go to the rock concert tonight."

"I hate rock music," Loretta said.

We stood looking through the screened door at each other, and this is hard to describe, fellow scientists, but as I looked, Loretta grew taller. It was an uncanny experience to watch her add two or three inches to her height right before my eyes. I was fascinated, even though it made the discrepancy in our heights even worse. Then I realized with a very unpleasant jolt that Loretta wasn't taller. I was shorter.

I became aware that Loretta was looking at me with . . . what? Pity? Perplexity? Scientific curiosity?

"Wait a minute," she said. She disappeared and came running back carrying a blanket and a bag.

"I brought us a snack," she said.

It seemed we had a date, after all. The trouble was, I had too much on my mind now to appreciate it.

I was shrinking. I was sure of it. Loretta seemed to loom over me. I rolled up my pant legs, tightened my belt a notch, and we headed for the park.

Loretta kept glancing at me, but she didn't say anything. I couldn't have answered her if she had. I could only listen to the flop-flop of my sneakers falling off my heels.

Once at the park it didn't matter if we talked, anyway. If you've ever been to a rock concert, you know what I mean.

And now we're sitting on Loretta's blanket, being menaced by Maynard Manning and his Rock Chompers, while my original uneasiness of mind turns into a horrible conviction.

Do you know what that conviction is, fellow scientists? Of course you do. We all know by now that Huey, red spot and all, was in that box, only he was too small to see. And since I drank the same loathsome mixture I forced on that poor, innocent animal, I am becoming small, too. The question is, How small am I going to become?

Fellow scientists, I don't want to be microscopic. I foresee too many problems, not the least of which is the risk of being stepped on. But aside from my selfish concerns, think of the loss to the world of science.

How small can you get, I wonder, and still retain your own personality and feelings? Will I keep going until I'm tiny enough to ride a paramecium? Or be eaten by one? Will I still be me when I'm too small to see? Oh, no. I'm beginning to sound like a Rock Chompers' song.

I have to suppress these morbid thoughts. I'm going to stop writing and listen to the music for a while. Maynard Manning is up there raging into the microphone. I'll try to understand the lyrics. My problems should seem slight by contrast.

Saturday, September 24

1:30 A.M.

Fellow truth seekers, don't start to read this until you are alone and at leisure. Once you begin, you won't be able to stop.

I'll start by saying that the books are closed on the Growth Encourager experiment. I'm still here. So is Huey, and we owe it all to Loretta. Well, not all. But quite a bit.

I would have figured it out eventually, probably. However, Loretta was in a calmer condition than I was, and she put her finger on the problem at once. I know you're eager to know all, fellow scientists, so here's the story.

When I stopped writing to listen to the music, the music stopped. The Rock Chompers were showing their audience a little mercy by taking a fifteen-minute break to stand around looking mean.

It was awkward at first.When you've spent the first half hour of a date scribbling away in a notebook, it's not easy to just drop it and start making small talk. You feel you should give some explanation or excuse, so I said, "You're probably wondering what I've been writing about."

"Not really," Loretta said.

Next to "so what," "not really" is my least favorite response. It leaves you with something to say and nobody to say it to. I was still trying to come up with my next line when Loretta said, "It has to be about how you shrank up all of a sudden."

Loretta does not pussyfoot around a subject.

"Oh," I said, "you noticed."

"Why do you think I'm here?" she asked. "To have my eardrums splintered?"

"Because you like short men?" I asked hopefully, but she said, "Because I want to know how you did it."

Somehow, since she was so matter-of-fact, I found myself telling all.

"You're kidding," she said, and "Get serious," and "You must be crazy." She couldn't seem to understand my motive. But she never said, "So what?"

I tried to explain. "You've never seen how I act with a taller girl."

"You're acting all right," she said.

I realized it was true. Worry had driven out silliness. I was behaving normally, even though I was shorter than ever. Somehow that gave me the courage to face what had to be faced, even if it was a hungry paramecium.

"Now that you know everything," I said, "I have an important request. If I become too small to hold this pencil, will you tell the world through my journal that I shrank like a man?"

"You're not shrinking," Loretta said. "You got shorter all at once and then you stabilized."

I checked my pant-leg length. She was right.

"But with proportionally the same dosage I took, the mouse disappeared. I can't understand it. I should have disappeared, too, not that I'm complaining," I said. I pulled the formula pages out of my notebook, murmuring, "Excuse me. I've got to go over this once more."

"You had that with you all this time?" She snatched the pages away and went through them quickly. To her credit she seemed to comprehend it all perfectly. To my credit I'm a neat and careful recorder.

Suddenly she said, "There's something wrong here."

"Where?" I asked, finding it hard to believe, although the fact that Huey and I were smaller instead of larger did seem to hint at an error somewhere.

"Here," she said, "where you subtracted 10 from 100 and got 990."

"That's not 100," I said. "It's 1000."

"It's 100," she insisted. "That other zero is a hole."

A hole! I looked closer. It was a hole, all right, a small, round, zero-looking hole made by either a tooth or a claw. Fellow scientists, Toodles had struck again!

The Rock Chompers were making threatening sounds on their guitars preparatory to another assault on our senses when Loretta stood up and said, "Come on."

"Where?" I asked. I didn't want to walk very far in floppy sneakers.

"Your place," Loretta said.

My heart soared. Loretta cared. She wanted to be alone with me in my time of trouble and shortness. I took a deep breath. "Loretta—" I began.

"It's still early," Loretta cut in. "We have time to work up another batch of Growth Encourager before I have to go home."

There was a definite lack of sympathy in her tone. It wasn't love for Zack Longwood that was motivating her; it was love of lab work.

"This is going to be fun," she said without a glance at the couple-strewn blankets we passed as we left the park. She seemed to have forgotten that to me it wasn't fun, it was life and death. Or at least height and width. To her it was just an interesting experiment.

For the first time I saw things from the point of view of the mice. But I won't allow bitterness to cloud our relationship. Her scientific bent is why I fell in love with Loretta in the first place.

Nobody was home when we got there, including Toodles. It made things much easier not to have to explain to my parents or contend with the mousehound.

As I expected, the error Loretta found was the only error in the whole experiment. Pretty good work, although I'll admit it was a rather crucial mistake. I was sure the corrected formula would result in the real Growth Encourager, but, fellow scientists, I have a confession to make. When the time came to swallow the formula, I couldn't do it.

For one thing there was no control to try it out on. Huey was gone, or at least not visible. It wasn't that I'd begun to doubt my competence, but I would have felt a lot better if I could see how it affected him first. I thought of using it on one of the other mice, but since they hadn't had the prior dose, their reactions wouldn't be conclusive.

Besides that, the taste of the stuff is indescribable. If there is ever a market for something utterly, unspeakably, sickeningly vile to the taste buds, my fortune will be made.

I got the test tube to my lips and smelled that special Growth Encourager smell, and I couldn't get any further. I don't know what Toodles sees in it.

"Hold your nose," Loretta suggested. "Shut your eyes. Hold your breath. Stand on one foot."

I tried each suggestion, even the last one. Nothing worked.

We sat there staring at the test tube.

"I take medicine with applesauce sometimes," Loretta said.

It was worth a try.

"This will probably turn out to be just a waste of applesauce." That's what I was starting to say when we entered the kitchen, but I never finished the sentence, because there in a fishbowl on the counter was Huey. He was tiny, much smaller than Dewey and Louie, but I'd have known him anywhere, even without the red spot on his back, by the way he scrambled all over the sides of the bowl trying to get away when he saw me and that test tube of formula. He may have been small, but his memory was as big as ever.

Now I didn't have to be my own guinea pig. Huey could take the first taste of the corrected Growth Encourager. He looked so frantic that I asked Loretta to get him out of the bowl. I was afraid he might faint if I touched him.

Loretta seemed to feel sorrier for the mouse than she did for me.

"Let's blindfold him," she said. "When he looks at you, he quivers all over."

"Just open his mouth," I told her, "and keep away from his teeth."

I squeezed the eyedropper in the test tube and held it over Huey's mouth.

"Ouch!" Loretta yelled.

She dropped the mouse. He grazed the test tube on his way down and hit the floor covered with Growth Encourager.

"He bit me," Loretta said.

"I told you to keep away from his teeth," I reminded her.

"You told me to open his mouth, and that's where his teeth happen to be," Loretta said.

Our first quarrel. But I didn't have time to try to win it.

"We have to catch the mouse," I said. "It won't be easy."

Loretta pointed to the floor. Huey hadn't even tried to run. He was flopping all over the place, licking his fur and rolling his red eyes.

"We've got to get that stuff off him," Loretta said.

She picked him up and washed him in the sink, and then we took him back to the basement to wait for results. We decided not to give him any more Growth Encourager. He'd swallowed enough accidentally, and the way he felt about me, I couldn't risk having him grow too big, you know what I mean?

While we waited, I showed Loretta around my lab,

which I'll have to admit took about two minutes, but I could tell she was very interested.

"If my mother knew about this, she wouldn't let me see you anymore," she said.

I perked up. It sounded as if Loretta hadn't written me off. I'd begun to fear that if I grew back to normal height, she would lose interest.

"Your mother has nothing to fear," I assured her. "In the right hands all of these chemicals are quite safe."

"It's not the chemicals," Loretta said. "My mother doesn't like chemists."

That seemed odd.

"Or scientists or experimenters or inventors," she added.

Odder still.

"Then why did she arrange a date for you and me?" I asked.

"She wants me to date ordinary, average boys," Loretta said. "She said you sounded very ordinary."

I could have laughed at her error. Me, ordinary? Me, average? Ha.

"She asked me if I played the guitar," I said.

Loretta nodded. "She feels a guitar player would be unlikely to be scientific."

Mentally I ran through the guitar players I had known. Her theory seemed valid.

"She'd probably be crazy about Main Man," I thought out loud.

"She would," Loretta said. "But I'm not."

My heart breathed a sigh of relief, but I had to ask. "Why not?"

"Because he doesn't interest me," Loretta said.

That's how unique Loretta is, fellow scientists. Not because he's too short or too tall or too ugly. She's interested (or in this case, not interested) in a man's mind. If I'd only waited, she would have found herself irresistibly attracted to me.

"Why doesn't your mother like scientific types?" I asked, confident that if she was anything like Loretta, I would have her under my spell in no time.

"Because of the time machine, for one thing," Loretta said.

"Time machine?" Did she say time machine? She couldn't have said time machine. But she did say time machine.

My pulse began to race in a reckless manner. I told myself to be reasonable. The words might not have the same meaning for her that they did for me. She was probably talking about some kind of clock.

Striving for calm, I said, "You wouldn't mean the kind of time machine that sends people backward or forward in time and then brings them home again, would you?"

"Something like that," Loretta said. "Except it didn't bring the cat back."

Normally I would have felt some sympathy for this cat, whoever it was, but I'll have to admit, fellow scientists, at that moment all my thoughts were on the time machine.

Naturally I've dabbled in time machinery over the years. I'm sure every thinking scientist has. But I never got anywhere, even as far as losing a cat.

I had a million questions to ask. The trouble was, I

tried to ask them all at once. They came out something like, "What, where, when, how, who?" It didn't matter. Loretta wasn't listening, anyway. She was staring at Huey and saying, "Look at the mouse."

"Forget the mouse," I said.

She looked at me in surprise. "He just grew. Don't you care?"

You know, fellow scientists, at that moment I didn't care. I was bored with the whole experiment. I didn't care if I stayed short or grew ten feet. I didn't even care about impressing Loretta. I just wanted to hear more about the time machine.

That's not like me, but a time machine is not your everyday invention, either. Just to get it over with, I grabbed the test tube and drained the rest of the formula.

"Zack!" Loretta said. "What are you doing?"

I couldn't answer. It took everything I had not to run screaming up the wall and across the ceiling. Loretta watched with fascination as every degree of disgust there is crossed my face in quick succession.

While I was trying not to turn completely inside out with repugnance, Toodles came bustling down the stairs, wagging his tail and obviously all ready to drive me crazy as usual. When he saw me, he skidded to a stop and stared. You could see he knew something was wrong but he couldn't decide what it was.

"Parents must be home," I gasped at Loretta. "Get me drink. Take dog."

Loretta is wonderful in a crisis. She understood immediately, grabbed Toodles up, even though by then he was bouncing stiff-legged up and down and yipping his ear-piercing yip, and hotfooted it up the stairs.

It seemed like hours before she came back. I passed the time trying to fit my head under the faucet so that the water could run into my mouth. I should keep a glass down there. No, the necessity will never arise again, because I will never take that stuff again.

Loretta came downstairs with a pitcher of lemonade, two glasses, and some superfluous cookies.

"Your mother's nice," she said.

I was beyond chitchat. I downed a glass of lemonade.

"Better," I said. "More."

I downed another glass.

"She told me she had Huey in the fishbowl because he didn't look well. She was going to fatten him up," Loretta said. "She thinks you were neglecting him."

I tried talking and it worked. "The way she feels about those mice, it's a wonder she didn't report me to the SPCA."

Loretta was peering into the cage. "Huey just dropped over dead," she said.

"What?" I gasped. I'm not a gasper as a rule, but this seemed to be the night for it.

I pushed Loretta aside and looked. Huey was shredding paper with abandon. He had never looked chipperer. When I threw Loretta a reproachful look, she giggled.

It was obviously time to walk her home. She was overtired and losing her concentration. Besides, maybe I could get her to show me the time machine.

In leaving the house I was careful to avoid my mother. If she had gotten a look at me, I might have found myself being fattened up in a fishbowl.

Loretta's house was dark.

"Your mother must be in bed already," I said.

Loretta laughed and said, "I never know *where* my mother is."

That didn't seem like something to laugh about, but before I could come up with a more suitable reaction, we saw a light flash on in the basement. Loretta looked pleased.

"She just got home," she said.

We would have seen anyone who drove or walked up to the house. If Loretta's mother had just gotten home, she must have tunneled in. I began to muse.

I became aware that Loretta was saying good night.

"See you tomorrow," I said firmly, but she didn't promise. It didn't matter. I would get inside that house if I had to mail myself there in a crate.

She opened the door, and something orange streaked past us and up a nearby tree.

"Oh, good. Mom found the cat," Loretta said.

She went inside and I started home, glancing at the cat as I passed its tree. It was clinging to a limb, looking as if life had hit it with one surprise too many.

My musings accelerated. Loretta had said the time machine lost the cat. Then how did her mother get it back? How could I get a look at the machine? How could I wait until tomorrow to go back to Loretta's?

It occurred to me that I still didn't know anything about Loretta's home life. We hadn't had a normal get-acquainted-type first date. Obviously somebody in her family was an inventor. You don't get time machines from catalogs.

It suddenly came to me that I was no longer walking out of my sneakers and that I could feel cool air on my ankles. I stopped and rolled down my pant legs.

The Growth Encourager experience poor old Huey and I had been through seemed childish now. Why did I ever think being taller was important? Science is important. Research is important. *Time machines* are important. I could see a whole new field of challenge ahead of me.

I walked on home, back to normal and feeling ten feet tall.

SAME DAY, 7:45 A.M.

Good morning, fellow world changers. Even though I was up half the night writing the evening's events, I still beat the birds out of bed this morning. I was so keyed up when I got home that it was easy to sit up and write it all down. On reading it over, however, I seem to have rambled somewhat from the purely scientific to things of a more personal nature. I don't think I'll worry about it, though. By the time this journal is published, I'll be so famous that every scrap of information about even my earliest years will be eagerly sought. I just hope that I can remain as humble and unspoiled as I am today.

And now to the matter at hand. Fellow world shapers, do you have any idea what happens to a scientific genius who finds out that there is a working time machine three blocks away? I'll tell you what happens. He wakes up at dawn and has to practically tie himself in a chair to keep from going to the time machine's house and demanding entry.

I've checked Huey several times. If there were any ill effects, they aren't evident. I don't expect any problems, so I can forget the mouse and devote all my energies to my newest love—that time machine. I've got to see it. I've got to feel it, hear it, smell it, travel in it.

I can't stand it. Early as it is, I have to call Loretta.

SAME DAY, 8:00 A.M.

I called. Here's the conversation. Why is she making things so difficult for me?

LORETTA: Hello.

ME: Hi, Loretta, can I come over?

LORETTA: Zack?

ME: Yes, can I come over now?

LORETTA: Zack, it's only eight A.M.

ME: That's okay. It'll take me until eight-ten to get there.

LORETTA: It's really too early, Zack.

ME: You're right. How about eight-fifteen?

LORETTA: Well, why don't you come for lunch?

ME: Fine. Around nine?

LORETTA: Around noon.

ME: Around ten?

We compromised at eleven. That's nearly three hours away. I don't think I can wait.

I know I can't wait.

I'm going over there now.

SAME DAY, 8:30 A.M.

I'm here. I'm sitting on Loretta's steps, slightly early for our lunch date, but etiquette is not exactly my main concern right now.

On the other side of this door is a real time machine. It seems too wonderful to be true. Maybe it *is* too wonderful to be true. No, I must crush that thought. If anybody but Loretta had told me they had a time machine stashed away somewhere, I would be justified in expressing some doubt. But Loretta can be trusted. I know her sense of humor is slightly whimsical, such as when she told me the mouse had passed away, but that was different. I hope.

The paperboy just flung the morning paper at me. Well, reading it will give me something to do while I wait.

Scientists of the world, I have seen the time machine. I'm sure I have, in spite of what Loretta says. Let me describe today's visit.

As it turned out, I didn't get much of the paper read this morning. I'd only been there a few minutes when the door was opened by a very small, slightly hunched old man with a whole lot of white hair shooting out from his head and tiny glasses perched on his nose. He didn't seem at all surprised to find a strange teenage person sitting on his steps reading his newspaper.

"The news is good, I hope," he said.

I stood up and stared. I knew without a doubt that I was in the presence of the inventor of the time machine. If every scientist in the world was melted down and reformed into one typical specimen, it would be this man. He even had an unidentifiable foreign accent.

I felt like shouting, "Take me to your time machine!" but by an admirable effort of will I limited myself to, "Hi, I'm Zack Longwood. Is Loretta home?"

He invited me in. Evidently he doesn't have the same aversion to early visitors that Loretta has.

"I'm Loretta's grandfather," he said. "Loretta is in the workshop. Just run on down."

Run on down? Was it really going to be that easy? No guards? No vicious dogs or murderous henchmen standing in my way?

I suspected a trick. Maybe he wanted to use me in an experiment. Maybe send me out where he sent the cat. Well, so what? I would welcome the opportunity.

The man misunderstood my hesitation.

"It's that door," he said.

"I know. Thanks," I told him.

It occurs to me now that it's odd that I knew. I'd never been inside that house before. It didn't strike me at the time, because all I could think was that I was almost face-to-face with the object of my dreams. Life is funny, fellow scientists. Yesterday that would have meant Loretta.

The man smiled a vague inventor's smile at me and toddled away. I ran downstairs, my heart pounding against my ribs with both fists, for the historic confrontation.

The workshop was a disappointment. I'd been sure I would find the time machine there. Where else would you keep one—in the kitchen? I was hazy on what else I expected to see—tools, maybe lumber or sheet metal, possibly blueprints. I was even more hazy about what the time machine would look like, but I never doubted that I would know it when I saw it.

But this was just an ordinary basement, maybe a little more cluttered than most, with shelves lined with preserves and baskets of apples on the floor. One end of the room was taken up with a long table littered with beakers, assorted test tubes, and a Bunsen burner—Loretta's lab, obviously. Loretta was there, writing at a little desk.

"It can't be lunchtime already," she said, and I said, "Where's the time machine?"

A trifle abrupt, I'll admit, but I was in the grip of a

powerful emotion. The real scientists among you will understand.

"Well, Zack, to tell the truth—" Loretta began, but by then I had spotted it. At least I had spotted, tucked away in a corner, the only thing in the room that by any stretch of the imagination could be called a time machine. At that, you really had to stretch.

It was a big letdown at first. I didn't know what to expect, but I know what I didn't expect—a fugitive from an amusement park. This thing would have looked right at home on the Flying Saucer ride I used to love when I was little. You spun around and shot pretend ray guns at the other saucers.

As I examined it, though, I could see that this was no plaything. It was made all in one piece of some material I couldn't identify. It wasn't any metal I knew, but it wasn't plastic, either, or glass or wood. It was small, with no roof or doors, and the dashboard had only two gauges and a button on it. They were labeled with funny, unreadable symbols, but other than that the machine didn't look very complicated to operate.

"So," I said, "how does it work?"

Loretta looked at me. She started to say something, seemed to change her mind, then seemed to change it back again. While she was still wavering, a woman came running down the stairs, saying, "Did I leave a jar of preserves—"

She broke off when she saw me and looked cautious.

"Mom, this is Zack," Loretta said.

Loretta's mother gave me what I can only call a searching look. Maybe I seem more scientific in person than I do on the phone. If you'll recall, scientists are not Loretta's mother's favorite people.

She took up the question-and-answer routine she had started during the phone conversation when she made the date for me and Loretta. It was hard for me to concentrate, because my thoughts at that moment were with the machine in the corner, but luckily Loretta's mother doesn't expect detailed answers. Mostly I just said, "Um," with an occasional, "Well, I."

"How did you like the concert?" she asked.

"Um."

"That's Maynard Manning's band, you know."

"I, um."

"Are you a friend of his?"

"Well, I."

"We bought this house from the Mannings this summer."

"I, um."

"Such a nice boy. He plays the guitar. Did you say you played the guitar?" She looked at me hopefully. I hated to disappoint her.

"Well, actually, uh," I said.

"This was the band's practice room when the Mannings lived here," she told me, and I said, "I know."

There it is again, fellow scientists. Did you notice that I told Mrs. Bringhurst that I knew Maynard's band practiced in that basement? How do I know? Beats me.

Loretta finally broke in. "Zack is here for lunch."

"How nice," Mrs. Bringhurst said. "We'll have

those preserves I got yesterday."

She walked over and picked up the jar from the seat of the time machine.

"Now, how did they get here?" she asked, but she didn't sound surprised at all. "I'll call you when it's ready," she said.

She gave Loretta a look as she started up the stairs. Fellow scientists, I could read that look as clearly as if she had spoken out loud. The look said, "Loretta, if you tell that kid about our secret time machine, I'll break your neck."

Hoping I was wrong, I went on as if we hadn't been interrupted.

"So," I said, "how does your time machine work?"

"Oh, Zack, didn't you know I was kidding?" Loretta said.

So I hadn't misread the look. The time machine was not to be discussed. I considered threats and violence and dismissed them. The sneaky approach seemed to offer a better chance of success. Cleverly I engaged Loretta in a seemingly safe and innocuous conversation.

"Well, I'm my normal size again," I said.

"I noticed," Loretta said. "How's Huey?"

"Normal size," I said.

"And the other mice?"

"They're fine," I said. Then I threw in a trick question. "How's your cat?"

She fell for it. "Much better, but he hasn't been downstairs since."

I lunged. "Afraid he'll get taken on another trip back in time?"

She knew she had made a mistake, but she wouldn't admit it.

"Zack," she said, "the cat did not go back in time."

"Forward, then," I said.

"It didn't go anywhere," Loretta said. "There is no time machine. I made that up"—she paused and thought—"to help take your mind off your shrinking."

Fellow scientists, I only hope Loretta leads a blameless life, because she will never be able to lie herself out of anything. The more she denied the time machine, the more I knew there was one. I decided to try bargaining.

"Loretta," I said, "if you'll tell me about the time machine, I'll give you Huey."

"I don't want Huey," she said.

"I'll give you Dewey. Louie. The whole family."

"I don't want your mice," she said.

It's lucky her mother called us for lunch at that moment, because I was about to offer Toodles.

As we left the room I took a quick peep at the paper Loretta had been working on when I came downstairs. I couldn't read it. No, it wasn't sloppy handwriting. It seemed very neat, but it wasn't English. It wasn't any language or even any alphabet I've ever seen.

The page was covered with weird symbols and characters that I've seen in only one other place—on the dashboard of what I am now convinced really is the time machine. Fellow seekers, my future actions are unclear to me as yet, but you can bet your buttons on one thing. The next time I write in this book you will be reading the words of an experienced time traveler.

Sunday, September 25

10:00 A.M.

As you begin to read this entry, brace your-selves for a letdown. I have not voyaged out of the twentieth century. I know what I promised, fellow truth seekers, but choke down your disappointment and read on.

You might feel more hopeful knowing that I am writing these words while actually sitting in the time machine. It's true. And let me say that it is a tight fit. I wanted to describe the machine while I was in it, but when I'm in it, I can't see it. There's nowhere to hold the journal but on my knees, and since there is no legroom in here, my knees are practically in my face. I hope I can make out these notes later.

Loretta's grandfather let me in and sent me down-stairs again, but Loretta isn't here. I assumed she would assume I was coming over this morning, but it seems our assumptions are not in tune. I thought I would pass the time in preliminary study, until I get a chance to badger Loretta for a test drive.

Unfortunately, as I said, once you're in this thing, the only view you get is of kneecaps.

However, something very odd has been developing as I write. It was almost imperceptible at first, but now I feel a very definite tingly sensation running through my whole body. It's not a pleasant sensation, I might add. Something like holding on to an electric fence while going down the first hill of a roller coaster. A confused description, but at this moment my thoughts are not responsible for themselves. I think I had better try to pry myself out of here before something—

SAME DAY, 10:30 A.M.

Fellow scientists, I have just—
Recent events—
Something has happened that—
I want to say—

SAME DAY, 10:40 A.M.

Please excuse the previous entry, fellow scientists. The fact is that I have just been through an experience that would have snapped the sanity of a lesser man. In my case it merely left me briefly inarticulate and with a need to sit and stare into space for a few restorative moments. Now that my thoughts are marshaled, I feel ready to set them down in an orderly manner, but be forewarned: They won't make sense.

Look back at my last intelligible entry. Notice how it was abruptly broken off. That was not because I had just remembered a previous engagement. It was because I suddenly wasn't here anymore.

I hadn't moved. I was still sitting all scrooched up in the machine, and it was still parked in a corner of a room, but all at once it wasn't the same room. In the blink of an eye (sorry, I'm in no shape to search for original turns of phrase) I went from Loretta's cluttered workshop to a cold, dark room lit only by a lantern held aloft by a woman who seemed shocked—I might almost say horrified—to see me. When I tried to stand up, another woman with her yelled, "Don't get out!" She sounded so frantic that I sat back down, but before I could ask any questions, I was back here in Loretta's basement, still sitting in the machine.

I'm writing this at Loretta's desk and wrestling with the question of whether I should report this occurrence to anyone, and if so, who. I have a sneaking suspicion that I have messed something up, maybe put someone in danger. But how? All I did was sit in that silly machine. I didn't touch anything, I don't think.

To tell the truth, I'd rather not share my little adventure with anyone. I don't like to admit that I was prowling around down here by myself. I know Loretta's grandfather thought she was here when he sent me down. I should have gone right back upstairs, but the curiosity natural to one of my keen intellect overrode my normally strong ethical sense.

But what is there to tell, really? Maybe I imagined the whole thing. Even if I didn't, it happened in a matter of seconds. How important could it be?

My thoughts are becoming unmarshaled. Maybe a listing of events will help me to a clearer understanding of my situation.

1. Felt tingly while sitting in machine.
2. Found myself and machine in unfamiliar place.
3. Welcomed by two decidedly unwelcoming women.
4. I don't know whether to list this or not. I thought one of them yelled, "Reset it and send it back."
5. I don't know whether to list this, either. The woman doing the shouting looked like Loretta's mother.
6. I was back in Loretta's basement, and the tingly feeling was gone.

That's it. Does it mean anything? Numbers four and five bother me. Could that really have been Loretta's mother? Could she really have said what I thought?

I'd like to wait for Loretta to show up, but after reading over my list I know I have to do something. I'm going upstairs to see who I can scare up.

Sunday, September 25, on into Monday, September 26

(MIDDLE OF NIGHT)

Friends of science, I have made good my promise. You are reading the words of an adventurer who has traveled through the centuries back into the mists of time. Well, maybe not quite the mists, but one hundred years back, which isn't exactly yesterday.

If you notice a certain restraint to my enthusiasm, it's because I didn't get quite all I expected out of the experience. As a mind-opening, attitude-altering event, it left a lot to be desired, mainly because when it was happening, I didn't know it was happening.

I've got to try it again. The world needs me to make that trip. My powers of observation, data organizing, and conclusion drawing are unparalleled. But, of course, you know that.

The facts are these: The kiddie ride look-alike is definitely a time machine, and the strange trip I took was really a time trip, and the woman I saw really was Loretta's mother, and she really did say, "Reset it and send it back." Why do I ever doubt myself?

Having said that, I've said just about all I know so far. It seems that because of me, Mrs. Bringhurst was almost stranded a hundred years back in time, separated from her husband and daughter and the life she knew. And she's not taking it very well.

The intuitive sense of danger that sent me sprinting for assistance this morning was right on the button. You'd think Mrs. Bringhurst would be glad that my sense of guilt for snooping around didn't keep me from alerting the family that the time machine was acting up, but that's not the case. Instead of being grateful, she blames me.

I have to be honest. In a way I can see her point. But I'm trying not to.

I'd better record the sequence of events, even though it leaves more questions than answers.

Once I decided someone had to be told, I moved fast. I found Loretta's grandfather upstairs, writing at a desk (using the same time machine symbols Loretta uses, by the way), and blurted out my story. He jumped up all in a twitter, saying, "We must get help," a reaction that nearly put me in a matching twitter. If he couldn't help me, who could?

"Come," he said, and he led me up to the attic where we found stacks of books and folders, bunches of dried plant material hanging from the rafters, and Loretta using a watering can to douse a tableful of potted plants. She wasn't alone. A middle-aged man sat studying a leaf through a magnifying glass. I assumed, rightly as it turned out, that he was her father, but there was no time then for introductions.

Loretta's grandfather plunged right into my story.

In my opinion he was too excited to do a good job of reporting, but Loretta and her father grasped the situation immediately and we all ran downstairs as fast as our various ages would allow.

We gathered around the time machine, and the old man panted, "It's been so long, I didn't trust myself to reset it."

"I just hope she hasn't made any adjustments I don't know about," Loretta's father said.

"If there's a problem, Zack can help," Loretta offered. "He's a genius."

Although true, it was probably not the best remark under the circumstances.

"If there's a problem, Zack will *need* help," her father said, and he threw me a look that I was sorry I caught.

Luckily there wasn't a problem. Mr. Bringhurst adjusted the dials and said, "Stand back. I'm sending it out."

We all stood there for about a minute while I wondered what he had done, and then the machine was gone. Just like that. I understood then what had happened to me earlier, but I couldn't see why it happened. I hadn't touched the controls.

Loretta came close to me and whispered, "Don't worry. I'm sure Mom's at Aunt Maggie's."

I didn't see how anybody's Aunt Maggie would enter into this, but before I could respond, the machine was back. It didn't fly in or slowly materialize; it was just suddenly there. So was Mrs. Bringhurst. Before I had a chance to welcome her back from wherever she had been, she froze me with an icy glare and said, "Loretta, it's time for your friend to go home."

I went. It seemed like the best thing to do.

As Loretta walked me to the door I tried to apologize for putting her mother in danger.

"She wasn't really in danger," Loretta said. "I knew we'd get her back. She was with her sister."

Loretta seemed to be under the impression that she was making sense.

"Why would she use a time machine to visit her sister?" I asked.

"Aunt Maggie lives a hundred years ago," Loretta said. "She won't come here, so Mom has to go there."

"Loretta," Mrs. Bringhurst called in a somewhat threatening tone, and Loretta said, "See you in school tomorrow."

I found myself staring dazedly at the closed front door, saying, "Wait. Listen. Wait. Listen."

I'm still pretty dazed. That's the only thing that has kept me from pounding on Loretta's door and demanding answers. Making such remarks to someone of my questing nature and then walking away is cruel and unusual treatment. Loretta forgets that a genius is human—superior but human.

It's the middle of the night. My thoughts are running amok. To stave off any ungovernable impulses, I'll make a list of the things I want Loretta to tell me tomorrow, in order of urgency.

Urgent question number one: How does the machine work, where did it come from, why did it take off with me, where was I, why does Mrs. Bringhurst's sister (Aunt Maggie) live a hundred years ago?

They can't be ranked. They're all urgent.

Monday, September 26

4:30 P.M.

It was a long night, and a longer morning, but lunchtime and my chance to talk to Loretta finally came. The frowns of Main Man added an intriguing element of danger.

It's gratifying to realize that it never occurred to me to drop my pickle into Loretta's milk. Last week I couldn't have resisted. It's remarkable how little our height difference matters to me anymore. Poor Huey. His taste buds were sacrificed for nothing.

There was no time to waste. Lunch period at our school is ridiculously short. I started out by trying to explain how my time machine heist was purely inadvertent, but Loretta interrupted.

"I know that," she said. "I told my mother it was an innocent mistake."

It's wonderful to see the confidence I have inspired in this girl on such short acquaintance. Mrs. Bringhurst is another story entirely.

"She says we can't go out anymore," Loretta said.

And they say mothers know best. This is harsh punishment. I'm fully aware that I almost caused Mrs. Bringhurst to live out her life in a world without electricity. But at least she wouldn't have been with strangers.

I'll never find another girl with a time machine. It's

bad enough to be unlucky in love. Why do I have to be unlucky in science, too?

No, I do not love Loretta only for her time machine. That's just my pathetic attempt to find some humor in a desperate situation. Remember, I was first attracted to Loretta when I thought she was a mere chemist—and tall, at that.

"Mom thinks you're too interested in the time machine," Loretta said.

"Who wouldn't be?" I couldn't help asking. "They're not all that common, you know."

"Now you can see why she's so particular about who I go out with," Loretta said. "She's afraid of knowledge of the machine falling into the wrong hands."

I was wounded. "She thinks my hands would be the wrong hands?"

"She knows that someone with your background would recognize the possibilities of a machine like that," Loretta said.

Granted, fellow scientists, the potential for personal gain is phenomenal. Even I, with my pure scientific mind, can understand the temptation an ordinary man might feel.

"She thinks nonscientists would be much less of a danger," Loretta said.

"Guitar players, for instance," I suggested.

"Right," Loretta said, adding, "she says I should have known better than to tell you about the machine."

I had wondered about that, and now I asked, "How

did you happen to confide in a virtual stranger? You'd hardly had time yet to realize my sterling qualities."

I was joking, sort of, but Loretta answered me seriously.

"I'd had time," she said. "Remember that day in Chem lab? You came up and told me in a squeaky little voice that you hoped I liked the school. Nobody else said that to me."

I nodded, trying not to cringe at her description of my voice.

"But even more than that"—she stared dreamily at her apple—"you were so brave when you thought you were going to shrink up to nothing—writing in your notebook, worrying about getting it all down for posterity. It was very heroic." She sniffed at her apple and sighed. "I wanted to reward you, so I told you about the time machine."

She took a bite of apple. In some confusion I watched her chew. Loretta had never shown the romantic side of her nature before. I wanted to say something, but I had a feeling that the squeaky little voice might make a comeback, so I just grabbed her apple, took a bite, and handed it back.

Loretta took another bite. Our eyes locked. It was a significant moment, interrupted by the bell that told us we were late for class.

As you can see, I didn't get many answers, at least not to the questions on my urgent list. I did find out that Loretta's grandfather did not invent the time machine. So much for wild white hair and unusual accents. Her father didn't invent it, either. Neither did her mother, although she's the one who uses it all the time. When I asked Loretta where it came from, she said, "We've just always had it around."

Some family heirloom. Apparently it will take patience, tact, and subtlety to break the pact of silence Mrs. Bringhurst has forced on her daughter. I must start developing those attributes at once.

Tuesday, September 27

1:30 P.M.

I've got thirty-five minutes to kill, and what better way to spend it than describing today's lunch with Loretta.

I'm in English class, and I rarely listen in English class. Once you can speak, read, and write a language, what's left to learn?

I was determined to use patience, tact, and subtlety during today's discussion. I started off pretty well. I said, "How's your family?" and Loretta said, "Good," and then I lost my head and said, "How can I get a ride in the time machine?"

I didn't expect to learn patience right away, but I did have higher hopes for my tact and subtlety.

"Zack," Loretta said reproachfully, "you know I'm not supposed to talk about the time machine."

"I know," I said. "Talk about it, anyway."

Loretta looked at me sadly. "I want to, Zack," she said, "but I don't like to go against my mother like that."

Loyalty. I like that. It's a funny position to be in, when the very thing you admire in a person is the thing you're trying to talk her out of.

"Tell me about your family," I said, changing the subject with tact and subtlety. "Tell me how you developed an interest in chemistry. Then tell me how the time machine works."

I had done it again. That last sentence just slipped out, but instead of being mad, Loretta laughed. She's not only loyal; she also has a nice disposition.

"About my interest in chemistry," she said. "I spent a lot of time with my grandfather growing up. My father is a botanist. He spends all his time classifying ancient plants, and that didn't interest me."

My ears perked up. "Ancient plants?"

"And, as you know, my mother travels a lot," she continued, ignoring my question.

"Let's talk about that," I said, and Loretta said, "Now, Zack. Anyway, Grandpop introduced me to chemistry, and when I was older, he trained me to help him in his work."

Aha, I thought, those symbols they use must be some kind of advanced chemistry notations.

"So your grandfather is a chemist," I said.

"He's an anthropologist," Loretta said. "Chemistry is a hobby."

"An anthropologist?" I asked. "Shouldn't he be in a hogan someplace or a thatched hut?"

"His research is pretty much completed," Loretta said. "He's doing a book now."

"What culture did he study?" I asked, and was a little surprised at Loretta's evasive, "Um, I'm not sure." If she helps him with his work, surely she knows who he's studying.

That's something I'll have to look into when I've developed a little more tact and subtlety. As you can see, my patience is coming along nicely.

I was trying to think of another leading question

when Loretta, in a transparent attempt to change the subject, said, "The cat's gone again."

Since I am barely acquainted with the cat, this news didn't upset me, but it did give me an opening.

"How did it happen to go time traveling?" I asked, trying to make it sound as if I were more interested in the cat than its trip.

"He likes to sleep in the machine," Loretta said unsuspiciously. "He must have knocked the dials when he jumped in, and sent himself out."

"Sounds pretty unstable," I said, as if there were a standard for time machines.

"The cat?" asked Loretta.

I gave her a pained look. Levity and time machine talk don't mix.

"Oh, the machine," Loretta said. "It's old. It needs work. The dials are loose, for one thing."

"Is that what caused me to hurtle away?" I asked.

"No," Loretta said, "you just happened to sit in it when it was programmed to pick up my mother at Aunt Maggie's."

"A hundred years ago," I said, and she said, "That's right."

Getting information piecemeal like this is driving me crazy. While I mused on the phenomenon of a time machine that needs a tune-up, Loretta went on about the cat.

"The little girl next door was playing with him yesterday and he ran away," she said.

"He's probably just out killing birds somewhere," I said kindly, but Loretta wasn't comforted.

"He always comes home at night," she said. "Besides, he can't kill birds in a dress."

"Would you care to add the information necessary to make that remark comprehensible to me?" I asked politely, and Loretta laughed, even though she still looked worried.

"She put a doll dress and bonnet on him," she told me. "He hates that."

"Understandable," I said, but as I write these words I keep wondering why that description is so familiar. An orange cat in a dress and hat. Where have I seen—

SAME DAY, 2:00 P.M.

Sorry to dash away like that, avid readers, but I had to get a hall pass and then try to think up a reason for getting Loretta out of class. I found her in the art room, and I was so wrought up when I asked for her that the teacher sent her out without a question. I know she thought something serious had happened.

Loretta must have thought so, too. She came out looking apprehensive.

"Was it a blue dress and a ruffled hat?" I asked.

I had given Loretta credit for a much quicker wit than she showed just then. Her response was a blank stare.

"A long blue dress and a hat with a ruffle," I said. "Was it?"

"Was what?" Loretta asked.

"The cat," I said, my self-control hanging on by a thread. "What was it wearing when it disappeared?"

"Oh," she said. "Just doll clothes. A dress and bonnet. Why, do you think you saw it?"

My self-control broke loose and floated away. I began snapping out orders. "When you get home, find your neighbor. Verify her description of the cat's clothes. And set up an appointment for me with your mother. I'll be over tonight."

Now I'm back in English class controlling an urge to jump up and down and yell. You're going to find this hard to believe. I find it hard to believe myself, but when I look at the facts, I find it hard not to believe. When I tell you what I know, you'll find it hard not to believe, too, although I'll admit it's really hard to believe.

Don't bother rereading that last paragraph. It was written by a man on the tenterhooks of anticipation. I can't wait to get home and read my diary—the one I started when I was a little kid and kept religiously for about two weeks, and then intermittently for another few months, writing only when something of moment happened.

And what did I consider "of moment"? Finding an orange cat stumbling around in a blue dress and ruffled bonnet!

SAME DAY, 4:30 P.M.

I have the diary before me. Here is the ten-year-old entry I want Mrs. Bringhurst to hear. I hope you'll make allowance for its simple and unpolished style. Even geniuses were once children.

SETTEMBUR 26: I FOWNED A CAT. IT HAS ORRINGE FURR. IT HAS A HAT ON AND A BLEW DRESS, BUT IT DOZEN LIKE IT. I AM GONE TO KEEP THE CAT.

There you have it, fellow scientists. What does it say to you? I know you're scientists, but this is one time it's safe to jump to a conclusion.

This is more than a touching story of a boy and his cat. This is documented proof that Loretta's cat took one more unauthorized trip in the time machine—this time ten years back—where it met with its future rescuer, me.

Reading the entry brought the day back clearly. It was the only time I ever ran away from home. A small, harmless experiment involving household bleach and crayon shavings had gone awry, and I had been ordered to sit in a chair and consider what had happened to the rug. I rebelled. Unnoticed by my mother, I scampered away, recklessly crossing streets, unaccompanied for the first time in my life, until I happened upon a cat hiding under a bush at Loretta's house. Of course, it wasn't Loretta's house then. Although I didn't know him at the time, I was in front of the house of Maynard Manning.

The cat was tastefully attired, but obviously miserable. I'd been wanting a pet—this was before Toodles came along to blight my life—and this animal seemed put there just for me. I didn't consider that a stray cat was unlikely to be fully clothed. I was young, remember.

The cat tried to run, but it kept getting its hind legs caught in its skirt and falling over. I forgot all about running away. Much against its will, I lugged the cat home and undressed it, but instead of the show of gratitude I expected, it scratched me and refused to eat.

The next morning when I let it out, it took off and I never saw it again—until Friday night when it shot past me on its way up a tree. Of course, I never suspected at that time that it was the same cat. Who would?

It's remarkable the leaps your imagination can take. A few days ago I found the idea of a time machine incredible. Today the fact that as a small boy I came in contact with a future cat seems perfectly reasonable.

When I present this evidence to Mrs. Bringhurst, she will forgive me for anything she has mistakenly considered me guilty of. And it will be only natural to send me to retrieve the cat, since I know where it was.

Here's my plan for bringing the cat back to the present. Find out from Loretta's neighbor exactly when the cat disappeared. Then set the time machine so that it arrives in the Mannings' basement at the same moment ten years ago that the cat did. Scoop it up and bring it home. Simple?

Loretta has had enough time to prepare her mother for my visit. I will now go and confront her with my diary, making a friend for life out of the woman by rescuing her lost cat.

SAME DAY, 7:30 P.M.

A major disappointment, fellow scientists—Mrs. Bringhurst has gone after the cat herself. She said she couldn't expose me to the risks involved, but the only risk I can see is that a ten-years-younger Maynard Manning might be in his basement when the time machine arrives. I'd enjoy that—a chance to be taller than Main Man.

Although Mrs. Bringhurst wouldn't let me make the trip, she seems reconciled to my constant presence now. I think she realizes that if I was going to contact some foreign power about the machine, I would be busy with that and not wasting my time trying to bring her cat back to the here and now.

It turns out that my rescue plan wasn't feasible, due to my incomplete understanding of the way the machine works. The problem is that you can pick the year you want to visit, but not the day. If you leave here on September 27, you arrive at your destination on September 27. To be there when the cat got there, we would have to put off our trip until next year on September 26.

Mrs. Bringhurst says it's not worth waiting a whole year. She thinks that when the cat ran away from me, it ran straight back to where I picked it up. It's ten years ago and the Bringhursts don't live there yet, but the cat doesn't know that. Mrs. Bringhurst claims all she has to do is send herself back ten years, open the cellar door, and call, and the cat will come running. We'll soon know if she's right.

Watching her ready the machine for the trip was illuminating. Apparently, once you master the meanings of the symbols on the instruments, the rest is easy. You set the year indicator for the number of years into the past you want to travel, and the time indicator for how long you plan to stay. Then you push the activator button and away you go.

The machine whisks you away, gives you ten seconds to get out, and then comes back here. You run around and see the sights of whatever time you've sent yourself to, keeping in mind that you'd better be back when the machine comes to get you, because you've only got ten seconds to get back in.

You wouldn't know from looking at the machine that it is in use, which I consider an oversight on the part of the designer. It may seem like nit-picking when the whole concept of the machine is so advanced, but I think it needs a warning light or a buzzer—something to keep two people from trying to use the machine at the same time.

The ten-second exit limit seems to be cutting it pretty close, too, but Loretta explained that you can't have an empty time machine sitting around in another time. It would attract unwelcome, and possibly dangerous, attention. Also, if you happen to land in water or a hostile environment, ten seconds isn't too long to sit tight until the machine takes off again.

I'm writing to keep myself busy while Loretta and I wait for Mrs. Bringhurst to rejoin us. I know she'll have the cat—what could go wrong? Only that the Mannings could be in the basement, or the door could be locked, or the cat could have gone elsewhere, or I could have dated my diary wrong. How could I have thought there were no risks involved in this venture? I could list another dozen possible catastrophes. An active imagination is a curse. I only hope—

The machine is back. Mrs. Bringhurst is aboard, with cat.

SAME DAY, 9:00 P.M.

Although I offered to stay, Mrs. Bringhurst sent me home for dinner. I'm now in my basement lab, contemplating the possibility of developing a system that will alert potential travelers that the time machine is in use. The work is complicated by the fact that I have no idea of the power source of the machine. Since it's made of materials that are unknown to me, the fuel or whatever it takes to make it go is probably equally obscure.

Mrs. Bringhurst had no trouble at all getting the cat. She said it was hiding under a bush right where I told her and looked extremely relieved to see her. It had probably been mercilessly teased by little Maynard, but hung around the house because it was home, even though the wrong people were suddenly in residence.

Loretta and her mother both made a fuss over the

cat, who looked like all he wanted was a good night's sleep.

"We can't let him come down here anymore," Loretta said. "He'll just continue to send himself away."

Mrs. Bringhurst examined the controls. "I knew the activator was loose," she said. "That didn't worry me too much, because I thought if he did it again, he would just go back to Maggie's again. But look," she said, stepping back, "now the year regulator is loose, too." A look at the gauge didn't tell me anything, but she said, "See, it slipped over one notch and sent him back ten years instead of a hundred."

"You realize, don't you," Loretta said, "that if it hadn't been for Zack, we would never have gotten Snuggums back."

Snuggums. What kind of a cat would you call Snuggums? I was almost sorry I'd helped locate him.

Mrs. Bringhurst expressed reluctant, and somewhat tardy, gratitude.

"A ride in the time machine will be sufficient thanks," I said graciously, but it didn't work.

"You know enough about the machine as it is," she said.

"You can trust me," I assured her.

"You're too interested," she said.

"Any normal boy would be interested in a time machine," I countered.

"You're not a normal boy," she accused me. "You're a scientist."

"As a matter of fact," I said, "I'm a genius."

That's when she sent me home.

Friday, September 30

11:00 P.M.

I've done it, I think. Sorry not to keep you up-to-date on a daily basis, avid readers, but thinking and experimenting has taken every available minute, except for a few short breaks to eat, sleep, and feed the mice.

My schoolwork has suffered, but now that I'm finished with my time machine work, I can easily catch up with (and surpass) the class. Just one of the advantages of being a genius.

A week of intensive lunch periods (the only time I've been able to talk to Loretta) has given me a somewhat better understanding of the capabilities of the time machine, although getting information from Loretta is like pulling teeth. An example:

BUSINESSLIKE TONE: Tell me about the time machine.

CASUALLY: What do you want to know?

TINGE OF IMPATIENCE: Anything. Everything.

OFFHANDEDLY: It takes you on trips.

SUPPRESSING IRRITATION: I know that much, Loretta.

SHRUGGING: Well, that's what it does. It takes you on trips.

FIGHTING FOR CONTROL: You make it sound like just another recreational vehicle.

MILD SURPRISE: That's what they are. That's what they're built for.

SHARPLY: They? Are there others?

FIRMLY: I meant to say, "it."

You see what I'm up against. It's the old story: Familiarity breeds contempt. She's so used to having a time machine around the house, she sees it in the same light as a dishwasher.

I tried to wake her up. "Aside from some of my own work, it's the most remarkable invention I've ever seen," I told her, and she said, "It has its limitations."

I know I expressed some slight criticism myself, fellow scientists, but the fact remains that this is not an achievement to be taken lightly.

"It sends you through time," I reminded her, "and you complain of limitations."

"What do you call this?" she asked. "When you go on a trip, you land exactly where you leave from. That means if you leave from this room, you land in the same place in the same room, or if you want to go back to the days before the house was built, you'll land in a swamp or an Indian camp or a dinosaur wallow—whatever was in this spot at the time you go back to."

"A little research before the trip would protect the traveler from surprises," I said.

"A lot of research," she said. "You can't just jump in and push buttons."

Was this an allusion to my unexpected excursion to her Aunt Maggie's?

"I did not jump in and push buttons," I said stiffly, but she was already making her next point.

"And not being able to dial a particular day is very inconvenient," she complained.

I suppose she's right. Marvelous as the machine is, it does have limitations.

My biggest surprise was finding that the machine goes back in time only—not forward. I found it hard to absorb this new concept into my understanding of the vehicle—all the time machines I've ever known have gone either way. Of course, all the time machines I've ever known have been fictional. When I commented, Loretta said, "They felt no good could come of visiting the future."

An obvious slip. Or does she say these things merely to drive me crazy? Either way I had to ask, "Who is 'they'?"

"Don't you mean 'who *are* they'?" she asked, trying to throw me off the subject with a trivial grammatical point.

I took a deep, steadying breath and said, "I mean who is, or are, the 'they' you just mentioned?"

"When?" she asked.

I had a choice between putting a hammerlock on Loretta until she talked or dropping the subject. I decided on the latter option—this time. Loretta obviously knows more about the origin of the machine than she admits. Why won't she tell me?

However, I'm not a genius for nothing. Using what knowledge I've gleaned, I've been able to develop a warning system that will alert any potential users that the machine is on hold, waiting to retrieve a time traveler. I can't wait to get to Loretta's to see if it's compatible with the machine's power system. It's pretty late, though. I should probably wait at least until it's light. (Joke.)

Saturday, October 1

11:00 A.M.

It works as perfectly as I had hoped and expected. Just touching the side of the machine activates the sensors I attached. There is no more danger of accidentally interrupting someone else's trip.

Too bad Loretta's parents missed the demonstration. Her father was classifying plants as usual, and her mother was doing things with apples from Aunt Maggie's trees. She says they're better because they haven't been sprayed. Evidently they get most of their vegetables and fruits from a hundred years ago. Quarantine officials would be tearing out their hair if they knew.

After I was sure I had done my usual brilliant job on the warning system, I tightened the loose dials on the control panel and just generally put the machine in better condition. Loretta's grandfather was profuse in expressions of gratitude.

"I knew it needed things," he said, "but being a simple anthropologist, I didn't know what to do."

"Just a few general maintenance procedures," I said. "I don't know enough about the machine to give it the thorough overhaul it needs."

Hint, hint, but it didn't work. I'm almost beginning to believe the claim that nobody in this family really knows any more about the machine than how to drive it.

Loretta's grandfather kept looking at me, even as I modestly disclaimed any real mechanical miracles. Anytime I glanced at him, I would catch his speculative stare. It made me so nervous that I came home earlier than I'd intended. It's time to head back, though. Mrs. Bringhurst is going after more apples, and I want to test my new system while the machine is actually in operation.

SAME DAY, 6:00 P.M.

Did you ever have the feeling that everybody knows what is going on but you? And that everybody knows you don't know what is going on, but they won't tell you? And that nobody wants you to know what is going on, and even if you guessed, they would deny it?

It's a lonely feeling, fellow scientists.

I should be thrilled by today's startling developments, but my excitement is tempered by the feeling that I don't really understand their significance.

When I went back to check the machine's performance during Mrs. Bringhurst's apple-picking jaunt, Loretta's grandfather met me at the door.

"Loretta is helping her father," he said, but he didn't call her. Instead he headed for the basement stairs and beckoned, so I followed.

Mrs. Bringhurst was already gone. The little warning light I installed this morning was glowing faithfully, and when I touched the machine, a buzzer buzzed. I'd prefer a more time machine-ish sound—something muted and faintly echoing, maybe—but I had to use the materials at hand.

Loretta's grandfather was looking at me speculatively again.

"You seem much smarter than the average human," he said.

His English is somewhat stilted, you'll notice, but I can't help agreeing with his sentiments.

"And you're able to keep a secret, too," he said.

"You can trust me implicitly," I told him.

It's heartening to know that a second member of this family has come to appreciate my finer qualities.

The old man nodded—to me or himself, I couldn't be sure—and then he ambled over to a corner of the basement and slipped a tarpaulin off—are you ready for this, fellow scientists?—another time machine!

"Do you think you could fix this?" he asked, as if we were looking at a bike with a flat.

Instead of fainting with excitement, I said in my most manly tone, "What seems to be the problem?"

"It won't go," he said, and I saw he wasn't going to be a whole lot of help.

"If I knew something of its construction and power system—" I prompted, without much hope.

He shrugged. "It was issued to me a long time ago," he said vaguely. "I only used it once."

Did he really mean "issued," or was it just the best verb he could come up with? I wanted to question him further, but he seemed to be waiting for me to do

83

something, so I went over and began examining the machine with what I hoped was a knowledgeable expression on my face.

This vehicle is a step up from the first one. The two appear to be made of the same material, whatever it is, but there the resemblance ends. To enter Mrs. Bringhurst's time machine you simply step over the side, but this is an enclosed, two-door model. It's fitted out with two comfortable-looking seats, as opposed to the molded form you perch on in the other machine. It even has storage space behind the seats— lots of it. You could stash the other time machine in there and still have room left over. It seems to be intended for more leisurely time travel, if there is such a thing.

I asked Loretta's grandfather if it was safe to get in, and he assured me it wouldn't go anyplace and neither would I.

"I've tried many times," he said sadly. "It's dead as a doornail."

I opened the door and slid in, being careful not to knock the control panel. The next time I visit the past, I want to be prepared.

The seats are as comfortable as they look, but the way the body is designed, you could never get out in the requisite ten seconds. Maybe this one waits around for you.

In contrast to the other machine, this one has a control panel bristling with dials, gauges, levers, and buttons. The only thing they have in common is their alphabet, if that's what it is.

"Is that a language or a code?" I asked, not really

expecting any useful information, but the old man said, "It's Qerbik," and then his eyes bugged out as if he realized he had made a slip. "An ancient language," he explained nervously.

I've never heard of any language, ancient or modern, called Qerbik, but I said, "From one of the cultures you've studied?" and he said, "Yes. No. I beg your pardon?"

I was framing another question when the first time machine suddenly vanished, breaking my train of thought. Within seconds it was back, bringing a basket of apples and Mrs. Bringhurst, who showed that she has a way to go toward developing any real confidence in me when she jumped out of the car demanding, *"Now* what have you been doing?"

"I showed it to him," Loretta's grandfather said, probably saving me from being pelted with a bushel of nineteenth-century apples. In answer to her dismayed expression, he added, "I think he can help me."

Mrs. Bringhurst shook her head. "If someone gets this machine away from us, you'll never get home."

"If I don't get it fixed, I'll never get home, anyway," he said. "I must try." He took her hand and patted it comfortingly. "Don't worry, Eliza," he said. "I've studied these people. This one is trustwor—"

Just at this critical point they glanced over and caught my goggle-eyed interest in their conversation. They turned slightly away from me and continued talking, but suddenly I couldn't catch what they were saying. It wasn't that they were whispering, fellow scientists, and it wasn't that they were mumbling. The reason I couldn't understand them was because—

some of the less imaginative among you will scoff—
they switched from English to Qerbik.

Well, why not? English is not Loretta's grandfather's native tongue. It's even beginning to sound as
if the twentieth century is not his native century. He
writes notes in Qerbik. The time machine's control
panels are in Qerbik. Why shouldn't he speak it?

While they were still conferring unintelligibly,
Loretta came running down the stairs wanting to
know what we were all doing there.

"I have asked your friend to try to fix the time machine," her grandfather said.

She glanced at her mother's little machine in surprise and asked, "When did it break?"

"*This* time machine," her grandfather said, patting
the top of the vehicle in question.

Loretta looked at the machine he was patting and
then at her grandfather. The old man's eyebrows went
up and down, and Loretta giggled. If there was a joke,
I missed it, but I smiled and patted the time machine,
too. For some reason that broke everybody up.

That little incident disturbs me more now than it
did at the time. What was so funny?

Tomorrow's events may throw some light on the
joke. Loretta's grandfather and I are going to work on
the machine, which is a joke in itself. How can I fix
something when I don't even know how it works?
The old man has complete confidence in me, but I
feel that it's misplaced. Even genius has limits.

Did I really write that?

SAME DAY, 11:45 P.M.

I've been lying in bed developing a theory, fellow scientists, and I won't be able to sleep until I write it down.

You already know that I believe Qerbik is a viable language spoken by at least two people; namely, Loretta's mother and grandfather and possibly Loretta herself. I will go even further. I believe the machine was invented in ancient times by Qerbik-speaking people and that Loretta's grandfather is a lost member of the tribe.

Laugh if you must. But then think about it. Why couldn't some ancient civilization have developed its technology to the point where these inventions were possible? I know that archeologists have never dug up any time machines or any writings in Qerbik. That doesn't mean there weren't any, does it? And if Loretta's aunt could go live in the 1800s, Loretta's grandfather could come from Qerbik times to live now. Couldn't he?

You're right. The idea is ridiculous.

Sunday, October 2

2:30 A.M.

I'm still awake. I'm still thinking. Maybe it's because it's the middle of the night, but my theory makes sense to me again. Loretta's grandfather was extremely nervous when I questioned him about the word *Qerbik*. That could have been because I was getting close to a clue to the time machine's origins.

I should have grabbed him by the throat right then and made him talk. Too bad I'm such a nice guy.

But if he really is from times past and wants to get back, why doesn't he use the other machine? Can't it go back far enough?

I'm going to sleep. If I think anymore, my theory will begin to seem ridiculous again.

SAME DAY, 4:30 A.M.

It's almost morning. In a few hours I'm going to have to go to Loretta's and pretend to work on that time machine. I can't fix it. How could I have let the old man go on thinking that I could? Now I'll have to disappoint him. And Loretta.

Maybe things will look better in the morning. No, they'll look worse.

SAME DAY, 4:00 P.M.

Sensational news, fellow scientists! Just wait until you read this!

By an amazing stroke of luck—but I can't write about it now! I can't sit still! I need to swing on the chandelier or jump over the garage!

You'll begin to understand the state I'm in when I tell you that I just kissed Toodles.

SAME DAY, 4:10 P.M.

I've gained some control now, fellow scientists. I'm still inclined to go leaping skyward whenever I think of what's happened, but that won't interfere with this report. I can write between leaps.

The fact is, I fixed the time machine. Let me revise that statement. The time machine now works. And as my reward—Wheeeee!

SAME DAY, 4:15 P.M.

I beg your pardon, fellow scientists. Another excitement attack overcame me, but I think I'm going to be all right now. Let me just stick to a straight narration of today's remarkable events. You can add your own exclamations.

By the way, I should have kissed Toodles long ago. He won't come near me now. He just peers at me from around corners.

I arrived at Loretta's feeling extremely low. I knew I couldn't repair the time machine, but my protests were taken for modesty by Loretta and her grandfather. He looked so full of happy anticipation that I was sorry I had shown up at all. It would be easier to disappoint him from a distance than to watch his face when he began to realize that I wasn't going to be any help to him.

"Come, come," he said delightedly, and we settled ourselves side by side in machine number two. Loretta observed from her desk. She looked as proud as if I'd fixed it already.

The old man led me through the whole seemingly endless procedure of starting up the machine. Nothing happened, but then nothing was expected to happen. After all, it had been sitting around gathering dust for years.

"Well, what is your opinion?" he asked.

My opinion was that this whole performance was a waste of time, but I couldn't say it, so I asked him to explain to me exactly what he was doing at each step. In other words, I stalled for time.

He repeated the program, making sure I saw what levers he pushed and what knobs he turned and what gauges he checked. He even showed me what some of the Qerbik symbols meant. The result was the same as before—no result.

"Any ideas yet?" he asked, looking at me with total trust. I glanced at Loretta and she had the same look on her face. I couldn't stand it.

"I think I'd better go home now," I said.

"Go home?" the old man echoed blankly.

He wanted me to stay and do something. The longer I put off admitting my ignorance, the more let down he would be, but admitting ignorance doesn't come easily to me, so I said, "I should go home and think the problem out. Do some calculations. Draw some charts." I wasn't making any sense to myself, but apparently it sounded all right to him.

"Of course," he said, but he looked so forlorn that I offered to run through the start-up one more time.

He practically clapped his hands.

"Good. Good," he said, and he leaned back out of my way and watched attentively.

There was a lot to it, but my memory is of course phenomenal, and I whipped through the whole routine without a hitch until the last step, when I turned a knob to the right and immediately remembered I should have turned it left.

"Oops," I said, just as Loretta's grandfather sputtered, "No, that's wrong, oh, my goodness," and then there was a popping sound and the machine began to hum, and the whole room was filled with a bluish-white light.

Fellow scientists, if that experience taught me anything, it was the meaning of the term *scared stiff.* All I could do was stare straight ahead of me at the control panel with all those lights blinking at me. I didn't know whether we were still in the basement or if I had launched us into the crater of a volcano. And that eerie glow—was it coming from the air around us, the car, or (gulp) me?

I don't know how long it was before Loretta's voice penetrated my consciousness. "He did it, Grandpop!"

she was shouting. It sounded like happy shouting and gave me the courage to turn my head toward the old man.

I'll never forget that sight, fellow scientists. His hair was wilder than ever, and tears were pouring down his face, but when our eyes met, he smiled from ear to ear.

"Thank you, my boy," he said fervently.

His gratitude embarrassed me. You know as well as I do that I didn't do anything, except make a lucky error.

As we got out of the car, Loretta's mother came running down the stairs.

"He did it!" Loretta shouted one more time, and she threw her arms around me and kissed me. I can't attach too much personal meaning to it, however, because she also kissed her mother and her grandfather and the time machine.

Loretta's mother cried and hugged the old man. I was practically crying myself just from group hysteria.

"How can we ever thank you?" Loretta's mother quavered.

There was a pause—a long, meaningful pause.

Then I said—but I don't have to tell you what I said, do I? I didn't really have to say it to Loretta's mother, either.

My time-traveling voyage of exploration is tentatively set for this coming Saturday, if I can survive the wait. Actually six days isn't very long to decide where, or rather when, I want to go.

How will I ever make up my mind? The whole past is before me!

Monday, October 3

7:00 P.M.

Report from Loretta: Mrs. Bringhurst having second thoughts. Worrying about accidents and what my parents would think.

Leaving for Loretta's immediately to threaten, cajole, riot, or whatever it takes.

SAME DAY, 10:00 P.M.

The trip is still go, after some shameless pleading on my part. Mrs. Bringhurst said she will give me a definite day and time tomorrow. I still haven't decided what era I want to visit. Maybe back to the beginning, if that's possible. Just so I don't go back *before* the beginning.

Tuesday, October 4

10:30 P.M.

Well, scientists of the world, if you were hoping to read in future entries about our planet in its infancy, you can forget it. I was told tonight that I'm to repeat my trip to Loretta's Aunt Maggie's home, which means I'm going back only a hundred years. I was hoping for a more undocumented period, but when I hinted to that effect, Mrs. Bringhurst said, "I won't send you out among strangers. Maggie will take care of you and make sure you don't get into any trouble."

Great. A time trip with a tour guide. As if that wasn't enough of a restriction, I can only stay for two hours. Some expedition.

I never thought I would hear myself quibble about a chance to explore in days of yore, but as Loretta was walking me home I said, "I was hoping to break new ground—to see things never seen by human eyes."

Loretta was sympathetic but unencouraging. "Mom's always been afraid of the machine," she said. "She worries so much that my father cut down his collecting trips to once a year. And she says I can't use it until I'm eighteen. But I'm negotiating for sixteen."

When I pointed out that her mother travels all the time, Loretta said, "Just back home."

"How do you mean, back home?" I asked.

"You know," Loretta said. "Back then. I don't think she would have left if she hadn't known she could go back anytime."

This information was inconsistent with what I had understood about the family situation.

"You mean, your Aunt Maggie is where she belongs?" I asked. "I mean, she didn't leave here for there? I mean, your mother left there for here?" I couldn't seem to get my thoughts articulated.

"If you're asking me if this is Mom's home century," Loretta said, "it's not. Dad met her on a trip and they fell in love. Isn't that romantic?"

"I thought the time machine was your mother's," I said, ignoring her last remark as totally irrelevant.

"It's my grandfather's, but he never uses it," Loretta said.

Another inconsistency. If Loretta's mother was back in time, wouldn't her grandfather be back there, too?

"Where was your grandfather all this time?" I asked.

Loretta stiffened. I can only describe her expression as wary, although I couldn't see the occasion for wariness. "What's Grandpop got to do with it?" she asked.

"I was just wondering how your father had the use of his future father-in-law's time machine before they had even met," I said reasonably.

I saw Loretta relax. "Oh," she said. "Grandpop is Dad's father, not Mom's."

That explained it. I don't know why I assumed the old man was her mother's father. Probably because they both speak Qerbik. As a scientist, I should know not to make careless assumptions. Even geniuses have lapses, it seems.

We had reached my house, and now I was walking Loretta back home.

"So your mother is over a hundred years old," I mused.

Loretta laughed. "Technically, maybe."

"And your father met her on a trip," I mused on.

"He was collecting," Loretta said. "Mom was living here with her married sister—"

"Here?" I interrupted.

"In our house," Loretta said. "It's the same house Mom lived in before she moved to the twentieth century. When it went on the market this spring, we snapped it up. It's so much more convenient for my mother than where we lived before."

We were back at Loretta's by this time. I looked at the house with new eyes.

"While we're walking around here, your hundred-year-old family is walking around here, too," I reflected, awed by the idea.

"It's that way everywhere," Loretta said matter-of-factly.

It's no fun discussing revolutionary concepts with someone who thinks they're old stuff. I said good night and walked home with a headful of new perceptions.

Wednesday, October 5

9:00 P.M.

Today my mother asked me what I wanted for my birthday dinner. She always makes me something special, and then we have ice cream and cake. It's one of those rituals mothers never grow out of.

A symptom of the overstimulating life I've been living lately is that I had forgotten my birthday is Saturday. I usually keep better track of gift-possibility days.

I can't miss this dinner. Last year I was working in the garage when my mother called me. I had reached a critical point in a delicate experiment and couldn't leave it immediately, and then I got so involved that I forgot she had called me. I never thought of it again until I walked into the house several hours later. The table was cleared, the dishes were washed, and I was in the doghouse. There was nothing I could do but promise myself not to let it happen again.

So this year I've thoughtfully arranged to be a hundred years away at dinnertime.

I think I've gotten around it, though. I asked if I could have Loretta over for my birthday and if we could eat later because it would be more convenient for her. It wasn't a lie. It *will* be more convenient, because she'll be monitoring my trip to her Aunt Maggie's.

Two more full days and a partial day to wait. Even though I'll be chaperoned by Loretta's aunt, this trip is still an exhilarating prospect.

Saturday, October 8

7:00 A.M.

Today's the day, fellow scientists. Life will never be the same for any of us again. I know your excitement and anticipation almost match mine, and you can rest assured I won't let you down.

The next words you read will probably be the most important ever recorded in any scientific journal up to this time.

Sunday, October 9

1:00 A.M.

I've been. I'm back. The whole trip was such a fiasco, for a while I considered not recording it at all, but that wouldn't be scientific. Facts are facts, even if they're stupid. So I'll set down what happened as it unfortunately happened, and if you want to skip this section, go ahead. In fact, I wish you would.

I arrived at Loretta's full of anticipation and confidence—overconfidence, I should say. While Loretta's mother was giving me tediously precise instructions on the operation of the time machine, I was planning how I could give Aunt Maggie the slip and do some exploring on my own.

That must be why I made the mistake I did in setting the year-indicator dial. It looked so simple, but it was the first time I'd ever done it, so I probably should have used a little more care. I sometimes think I detect in myself a slight tendency toward hasty action.

But what's the use of berating myself? I'll just write what occurred and then put it behind me—if Loretta's mother will let me.

Everything was normal at first. The vibration, the tingle, the sudden arrival in a different environment. But it was the wrong environment. I knew right away that there was a mix-up, but with ten seconds to get out of the machine or get taken back home, there was no time for reflection.

The machine left me standing in the same basement I had just left, as expected, only there was no Aunt Maggie waiting with a lantern, and the basement wasn't the dark, cold cellar it had been in her time. But it wasn't the way the Bringhursts have it fixed up, either. No messy desk, no lab table, no time machines. Instead there were a piano, a drum set, and various guitars lying around.

I suddenly understood the flashback I had when I first saw this basement. It was a memory. When I told Mrs. Bringhurst I knew Main Man's band practiced here, it was because I had been here. I was remembering this trip. But how could I have a memory of something before it happened? Of course, I'm here now and it's before the memory, but there hadn't been anything to remember when I originally remembered. See what I mean? I don't, either.

I didn't have the leisure to explore these philosophical questions at the time, because I had hardly gotten my bearings when Maynard Manning himself came galloping down the stairs followed by several burly Rock Chompers.

"Hey, Longwood!" he growled. "What are you doing here?"

There was a general ominous murmur among the Chompers, and since I've never been on especially cordial terms with any of them, and since my answer to the question would do nothing toward improving relations, I decided to make tracks to the nearest exit, which was up a flight of stairs to the outside door.

As fleet of foot as I am swift of brain, I beat it out of there and on down the street while the band was still milling around their instruments, presumably looking for signs of vandalism or whatever they suspected me of.

Self-preservation was the only thing on my mind as I scooted for home, but at the last minute, instead of bursting through the front door, I ran around to the garage. If Manning and his boys were following me, I didn't want them to storm the house. My parents are touchy about things like that.

I didn't go into the garage, though, because it was already occupied. A boy was standing with his back toward me, absorbed in transferring some bubbly blue stuff from a beaker to a test tube. I sneaked around the corner of the garage and looked in the window. What I saw made me throw myself back against the wall and slowly sink to the ground, wide of eyes and slack of jaw. Fellow scientists, it was me in there.

I was sitting quietly, trying to get over the shock of meeting myself face-to-face without a mirror when I heard my mother calling. You'll know I still didn't have a good grip on the situation when I tell you that I almost answered her before I heard the other Zack yell, "Here I am."

I was afraid to look in the window again, but I could tell that Mom went into the garage. I could hear her talking to me/him.

"Dinner's ready, birthday boy," she said.

"Five minutes, okay?" I/he mumbled, and she said, "Five minutes," and left.

That's when the horrible truth climbed up on my

shoulder and giggled in my face. I was in the past, all right, but it wasn't the distant past by a long shot. A few facts made the year easy to figure:

1. The Mannings were still living in Loretta's house.
2. I was still using the garage as my lab.
3. My mother was calling me to my birthday dinner.

Of the three of us, only I knew that the birthday boy was not going to make his birthday dinner. You know it, too, don't you, fellow scientists? You have already guessed what I'm forced to admit now, whatever the cost to my self-esteem.

By careless manipulation of the time machine's controls I sent myself back in time exactly (choke) one year.

One year. An hour with Aunt Maggie would be more of an adventure than that. I wanted a journey to the dawn of history, not a trip down memory lane. Resisting a strong urge to bang my head against the garage wall, I took another peek through the window.

The solution in the test tube was starting to smoke. I remembered the occasion so well. It was a sensitive moment, one that you couldn't put on hold and come back to later. That's why I missed the dinner.

Well, there was nothing to be done about it now. Aunt Maggie, lantern aloft, would wait in the cellar in vain while I relived last year's experiment.

I began to consider how to put in the time until the machine was due to pick me up for the return trip. I refused to worry yet about how I was going to get back into the Mannings' basement. Why subject myself to abject terror before it was absolutely necessary?

I had almost two hours to spend here in last year, and I didn't want to spend it skulking around the garage, but where could I go? My own house was out of bounds, and I couldn't walk around the neighborhood for fear of encountering one of the mad musicians.

The need for a quick decision became acute when Toodles came sniffing around the corner, playing watchdog. When he saw me, he stood as still as a snake, with his nose wiggling like a rabbit's. He leaned down and sniffed, and he stood tall and sniffed. He ducked back out of sight for a minute, and I knew he was looking at the Zack in the garage. Then he came back and looked at me again. It would have been funny if it hadn't been serious.

I could see it was only a matter of time before he started barking his furry little head off, so, hoping to reassure him, I murmured, "Hi, Toodles, good boy," in a friendly tone, but it was a mistake. Maybe I'd never spoken to him in a friendly tone before. He started barking his piercing barks and making little growling rushes toward me, keeping just out of reach.

"Down," I said. "Heel. Sit. Quiet," but it's hard to sound firm in an undertone, and Toodles had himself in such a state by that time, I don't think he heard me, anyway.

My mother heard the racket and came out to see what was going on.

"What did you do to Toodles?" she asked.

Typical. Even on my birthday she sides with Toodles.

"Nothing," I said, which for once was perfectly true, although if she had come out two minutes later, she might have had something to complain about.

"Well, come on in before everything is cold," she said, and to keep her away from the garage I accompanied her into the house.

My father was already at the table. "We were afraid you weren't going to make it," he said with a big smile. I could see that no such thought had really crossed his mind.

It's funny, but I had never realized before how much this "Happy Birthday Zack" stuff meant to my parents. I always thought of it as something they did for *me*. Until that moment I hadn't understood that by being there and enjoying myself I was doing something for *them*.

So in spite of Toodles growling in the corner and giving me dirty looks, I relaxed and enjoyed the meal and the conversation, although to me some of the topics were a little out of date.

I had a few uneasy moments, but nothing serious. Nobody noticed my change of clothes—luckily my T-shirts don't say anything memorable. When my mother remarked that I seemed older already, I had a slight coughing spell, but other than that it was a great dinner, topped off by ice cream and a cake that was short one candle, if they only knew it.

I was enjoying myself so much, in fact, that time sort of ran away from me. Mom was telling me how adorable I was at every stage of my development when I suddenly realized that I only had about twenty minutes to sneak or talk my way into Main Man's basement.

I sat there hiding my growing tenseness while I tried to think of some graceful way to leave. I *had* to be back in the basement when the time machine came back for me. If I missed it, nobody would send it back again, because nobody knew where I was.

I didn't want to stay in last year for always. Even if my parents and Toodles accepted me, I knew I wouldn't like being my own big brother. Or my own little brother, either.

"Well," I said with admirable calm, "I hate to break this up, but I'd better check on my experiment."

"You and your experiments," my mother said fondly. She usually says that phrase in a very different tone, but it was my birthday.

I walked around the table and kissed my parents.

"Thanks for everything, guys," I said.

We all smiled at each other, and right at that moment, sending myself back one year didn't seem like such a mistake, after all.

My dignified departure was somewhat marred by the fact that Toodles was hanging on to my pant leg with all his teeth. When I got outside, I separated his mouth from the material and took off running toward Manning's.

It had gotten dark while we were eating, which made me feel safer about approaching the house, but I didn't have to worry, because nobody was outside. The door I had escaped through was ajar, not enough to see inside but enough so that I could hear voices. It sounded like the whole band in there, and they were either arguing or singing. When I realized I could understand their words, I knew they weren't singing.

"Come on, get serious," Maynard was saying. "This band needs a name."

There was a babble of suggestions, all goofy, but you could see the image they wanted to project—tough and mean. Why, I don't know, unless they hoped to scare people into listening to their music.

The discussion was getting heated, and my time was running out when a hand clutched me by the back of the neck and dragged me through the door and down the stairs.

I was surprised when I was able to twist around and see that it was one of the band members who had grabbed me. I would have expected a musician's hands to have a lighter touch.

I was immediately encircled by menacing guitar players, but any trepidation I might have felt was overriden by the realization that in one minute the time machine was due to land in the corner approximately three yards from where I stood, and if I wanted to go anywhere, I had to be waiting in that corner when it arrived.

"What are you after, Longwood?" Main Man growled.

Fellow scientists, the idea that came to me then was ingenious, even for a genius.

"I've got a name for your band," I said.

There was no reaction. Their expressions seemed to

say that they were more interested in tearing me apart than naming their band.

"Listen to this," I said desperately. "The Rock Chompers."

It was like saying the magic word. The band's lips moved in unison as they tried out the sound. Then they all looked at each other in amazement, while I looked at the steps down which Toodles was charging, teeth ready for action. It had taken him a while, but he had caught up with me.

The new Rock Chompers were shouting, "That's it!" but I couldn't hang around to listen to their touching expressions of gratitude. I broke through the circle and ran for the time machine stop. My timing was perfect. So was Toodles's. He wrapped his teeth around my ankle just as the time machine materialized around us and whisked us back into next year.

Loretta, her mother, and her grandfather were waiting to welcome me back.

"A dog," the old man said wonderingly.

"It looks just like Toodles," Loretta said.

"It *is* Toodles, as a matter of fact," I said, and to spare everybody any suspense, I launched immediately into my explanation. "First of all," I began, "I didn't quite make it to Aunt Maggie's."

"What?" Mrs. Bringhurst shouted. She continued to shout "What?" at intervals during my story, making it a little difficult to concentrate, but I did try to stress the more positive aspects of the venture and not dwell too much on the basic errors that were made.

Mrs. Bringhurst, however, seemed to be able to absorb only two facts—that I had gone to the wrong century and that I had brought back a dog. My offer to return Toodles met with swift and definite rejection.

Rather than repeat her somewhat detailed criticism of my actions and level of maturity, I will only say that unless I can think of something to change Mrs. Bringhurst's attitude, there are no more trips to the past in my future. She is going to go back late tonight, when the Chompers have dispersed, to return Toodles. When Loretta and I left, he had given up trying to separate me from my ankle and was busy checking out everything in the basement with his nose. Loretta was allowed to come to my birthday dinner, so Mrs. Bringhurst hasn't rejected me as a person, just as a time traveler.

At dinner I couldn't resist a little memory experiment.

"This is delicious, Mom," I said. "Even better than last year."

"Last year?" she said. "You didn't make it last year, remember?"

I watched with interest as she stopped in mid-bite, looking thoughtful. "Why did I say that?" she murmured, and Loretta kicked me.

The birthday dinner was a success, and I could tell that both parents liked Loretta. My mother did remark on my less-than-hearty appetite, but since I'd already had one birthday dinner, it couldn't be helped.

Loretta has gone home now, my parents have been in bed for an hour, and even tireless Toodles is asleep with his chin on my foot.

Only my dedication to science has kept me awake long enough to get today's events down in black and white. As soon as I let in Toodles, who is whining and scratching at the door, I'll go to bed.

Wait a minute. Toodles? At the door? Oh, no—

SAME DAY, 10:00 A.M.

You can relax, fellow scientists. Everything is under control. I suffered through some nervous moments last night, but I managed to get everything worked out satisfactorily—well, almost satisfactorily.

As I feared, it really *was* Toodles scratching outside—the time-traveling Toodles, that is. When I opened the door, he bounded into the room and then stopped dead when he saw his double glaring at him from under the table.

The meeting of the two Toodleses might have been laughable if there wasn't so much at stake. I knew if my mother ever found out how I was yanking her baby back and forth among the years, my future tranquillity was doomed, so before anybody got the urge to bark, I tucked one Toodles under each arm and hustled them down to my lab.

There was a lot of hackle raising and showing of tiny fangs, and it didn't take long to see that the two dogs were incompatible. The problem is, they are different versions of the same dog, and it is a dog who absolutely has to have its own way. Words like *share*, *compromise,* and *concede* are not in this animal's vocabulary.

If one Toodles sniffed a mouse, the other one had to sniff the same mouse. If one sat down, the other pushed him over so he could sit in the same place. There were constant skirmishes, which I saw would soon lead to all-out war.

I decided that, late as it was, I would have to take last year's Toodles back to the Bringhursts'. An easy decision to make—not so easy to carry out, I discovered. The fact is, fellow scientists, I had lost track of which dog was which.

I know, I know, I should have marked the dogs. There is no excuse for such unscientific-ness. I keep reminding myself that I had a big day yesterday and it was late when Toodles dropped by, but it doesn't help, especially when I imagine the frowns and head shakings going on as you read this.

I did my best. I looked at their teeth and gazed into their eyes, but it wasn't easy to judge. Their fur hid any telltale wrinkles, and there's only one year's difference in their ages, anyway.

Finally I decided that one of them had a slightly more mature manner, so I left him upstairs (away from the mice) and took the other one back to Loretta's.

I didn't have to wake anybody up. The house was ablaze with lights, and when I knocked, Loretta's grandfather answered the door holding a huge soup bone.

"We're looking for Toodles," he said. "Oh, there he is."

He thrust the bone at him happily, but since it was almost as big as the dog, Toodles declined the gift.

Loretta came running up and pulled me into the house, and her parents came from different directions, looking irritated and relieved when they saw Toodles.

"We thought he was hiding in the house somewhere," Loretta said.

"Now that I'm here, I may as well take him back for you," I offered, but it didn't go over, so I handed Toodles to Loretta, said good night, and came on home.

I plan to stop in later this morning to hear how everything went, but I have no doubt that Toodles is back in the bosom of last year's Longwood family, bewildered but safe.

The trouble is, the more I look at the remaining Toodles, the more I wonder if I sent back the right dog. He often seems lost in thought, which is unusual, since Toodles has always been more active than reflective. And when I come near, he goes running for my mother.

It's something I'll have to learn to live with—the possibility that I returned the wrong dog, that I have condemned one Toodles to a year of déjà vu and the other to a twelve-month blank.

Well, that's easier to accept than the knowledge that I'm responsible for the name Rock Chompers.

SAME DAY, 4:00 P.M.

Fellow scientists, if you felt any uneasiness about Toodles, you can relax now. As I predicted, he was returned home last night without incident.

While I was there today, Mrs. Bringhurst was off visiting her sister, no doubt to explain my nonappearance. I can just hear them.

"Maggie, he may be a genius, but he hasn't got a lick of sense."

"Land sakes, Eliza, I'd have thought teenagers would have smartened up in a hundred years."

I'm glad I wasn't there.

As soon as I got to Loretta's, she told me her grandfather wanted to see me. I was a little worried that I might be in for a lecture about yesterday's sloppy science, but when I stuck my head in his door, he looked so pleased to see me, I knew it was okay.

What he wanted was to thank me another dozen times for fixing his machine and to tell me that he is going away.

"Back to Qerbik?" I asked, as if I knew all about the place.

"I see you have guessed that I am Qerbikan," he said. "That is good. There should be no secrets between us now. You have made it possible for me to spend my remaining hundred years among old friends and scenes of my childhood. Someday I will repay you, but at this time I can't tell you how."

He smiled and looked mysterious. I felt like saying, "No secrets, remember?" but he was enjoying himself too much. It seemed like a good time to ask some questions, though, so I said, "Have you been here a long time?"

"Most of my life," he said. "I had intended to spend a few years here and then move on, but as you know, problems arose." He spread out his hands and shrugged his shoulders.

"So you were stuck here," I said.

He nodded. "I have been happy," he said. "I found that I enjoyed the simple, primitive life, and of course I had my work and, later, my family. It seemed I would live out my days here." He gave me a fatherly pat on the head and continued, misty-eyed. "Now, thanks to you, I will see my home again. I will once more wander through the abloskeg when the yalex bloom. I will hear the song of the chermlot and the haunting call of the yakodor."

He stopped speaking and stood lost in memory. While he dreamed of blooming yalex, I ruminated on the idea that he considered today's way of life simple and primitive. And what was that about his next hundred years? He must be feeling pretty good.

He dragged his thoughts out of the abloskeg to say, "I want to say good-bye now. I might not see you before I leave."

He fumbled around on his desk until he came up with a small shiny object, which he handed me.

"This is to remember me by," he said.

I examined the object. It looked like a small metal box, but it didn't feel like metal, and it didn't seem to open. It had several buttons labeled in Qerbik, but when I touched them, nothing happened.

"What is it?" I asked.

"If you find out, you can let me know," the old man said with a Qerbik chuckle.

When I tried to say good-bye, he sent me off to find Loretta, saying, "We will meet again before long," but he didn't say if he meant there or here.

Loretta seemed kind of depressed. She couldn't be losing interest in me, could she? The very thought makes me feel short.

No, she must be feeling sad about her grandfather. It's nice to know he'll be happy, but still, it'll be a big change in her life.

I feel kind of depressed myself. It's hard to face a future with no time travel in it. Loretta's grandfather says we'll meet again, but how?

I wandered on home early, thinking I might do a little schoolwork. I'm still thinking about it.

Monday, October 10

4:30 P.M.

Was it only last night that I was depressed? Well, fellow scientists, my future has taken a definite turn for the better—I might even say, for the great. Opportunities are opening for me in every direction.

First, an unexpected result of my brief return to last year is that my relationship with the Rock Chompers has changed dramatically.

This morning they were lounging around on the school steps intimidating the arriving students as usual, but as I hurried by, instead of sticking out their feet to trip me, they eyed me with a kind of puzzled respect, and Main Man said, "Hey, Longwood, wait a minute."

I was hoping for an early-morning chat with Loretta, but when Main Man says, "Wait a minute," people are inclined to wait.

"I've always wanted to ask you . . ." He paused. "At least I think I've always wanted to ask you . . ." His mind seemed to wander for a moment, but then he said, "How did you and the dog get out of the room that night?"

There was no way to answer that question with any degree of truthfulness, so I said, "What night?"

"The night you named the band," he said.

From the other Chompers there came a deep chorus

of, "Great name, man," and "Good job, Longwood," and other words of approbation.

"A great name was all we needed to become a success," Main Man told me.

"That surprises me," I said. Actually, hearing that they were a success is what surprised me.

I was even more surprised when Maynard invited me to a practice session at his house. And I was as astonished as you are to hear myself promising to go.

At lunch I got a big wave from Main Man and guttural greetings from the Chompers, even though I was sitting with Loretta. She didn't seem to notice that Maynard had dropped out of the race for her affections. When she told me her grandfather had left last night, I understood why she was so subdued.

"Did he have any problem starting the machine?" I asked.

"No," she said. "The worst part was dragging the thing outside."

It didn't occur to me that I was about to hear something world-shaking. I just thought that they had gone to a lot of unnecessary trouble.

"Why outside?" I asked.

"So it wouldn't go through the roof," Loretta said.

I have to admit, fellow scientists, that I still didn't see it coming.

"Doesn't it just dissolve like the other one?" I asked.

Loretta choked, drank some milk, and said, lips twitching, "Zack, don't you know that wasn't a time machine?"

Still wrapped in ignorance, I said, "If it isn't a time

machine, how did your grandfather get home?"

By now Loretta was laughing herself silly. I would have been glad to see that her spirits had lifted, if her mirth hadn't been so obviously directed at me. She glanced at my unamused face and controlled herself enough to answer my question.

"He went home in his spaceship," she said.

Yes, fellow scientists, she said "spaceship." I waited to see if she would correct herself or add some clarifying remarks, but none were forthcoming. Loretta is obviously researching my breaking point, and this time she almost found it. Holding myself in check by a superhuman effort, I said, "Are you saying that Qerbik is not an ancient lost civilization?"

That set her off again. "Qerbik is a planet," she gasped.

Looking back, I can only admire the strength of character that allowed me to say in a calm, rational manner, "Loretta, if you don't stop laughing and tell me everything, speaking in paragraphs instead of sentences, you are going to be very, very sorry."

Loretta was unimpressed by my threat, but she did make an effort to get hold of herself. "I just told you everything," she said, wiping her eyes.

After consideration I had to admit that she had— everything that mattered, anyway. But I wanted details. Such as why she hadn't told me before this.

Her excuse was that she had been warned from the cradle never to let it slip that her grandfather was not a local product.

"Word would have gotten around," she said, "and Grandpop always hated a fuss."

The word *fuss* in this case was probably an understatement.

"But he wanted *you* to know," she went on. "In fact, he thought you had figured it out when you said you knew he was Qerbikan. He never dreamed you thought Qerbik was—"

To ward off another bout of giggles, I said, "He told me we'd meet again."

"He's going to arrange for you to visit Qerbik," Loretta said.

I shot up out of my seat shouting, "How? When?"

"I don't know, Zack," Loretta said. "Sit down."

I would have preferred to go on shouting, but I sat down and lowered my voice to give the other students an opportunity to go back to their own conversations.

"Soon?" I asked. "A week? A month? Tomorrow?"

"I don't know, Zack," Loretta repeated. "He just said he was going to make arrangements. I don't know what that involves."

"Wonderful," I said. "I'll just have to go from day to day wondering when a spaceship will land in my yard with 'Qerbik Express' written on it. Or am I supposed to build my own?"

I had intended sarcasm, but Loretta said, "I bet you could, Zack," with such sincerity that I forgave her for every fact she ever suppressed.

"It isn't that I'm not glad about the trip," I said. "It's just that I don't know how I'll stand the wait."

"You'll have plenty to do," Loretta said. "I'll teach you Qerbik."

"So you *do* speak it," I said.

"We spoke it at home so Grandpop wouldn't forget

it," she said. "He always hoped somehow he'd get home again. And now, thanks to you—"

There is no way to convince these Bringhursts that I didn't really fix the machine. To change the subject I reached in my pocket and pulled out the silver box the old man had given me.

"He left me this," I said.

Loretta's eyes opened wide. "His transmitter," she said. "Do you think you can fix it?"

"I doubt it," I said. "I didn't even know what it was."

Loretta took the transmitter and turned it over in her hands, smiling a little. "It might not even be broken," she said. "We couldn't figure out how to work it, and Grandpop couldn't remember." She handed it back to me. "They shouldn't have let him go off by himself," she said. "He's not mechanically inclined."

The bell ended our conference and now, aside from learning Qerbik, there is nothing to do but wait for whatever is going to happen. I'm wondering how to prepare my parents for my impending journey. If any of you have ever tried to tell a mother who won't even leave you home alone for a weekend that you are planning a space trip with an alien being, I'd like to hear from you.

I can't just sit around waiting. I need meaningful work to do. It won't be time machine work. Loretta's grandfather left the machine with Mrs. Bringhurst, but it will take time to regain her trust.

I'll look over the transmitter the old man left with me. I fixed the spaceship, didn't I? Maybe dumb luck will strike again.

Or I could get out my old transmutation of matter formula and see what I can do with it.

And it's time the mice started earning their keep.

There's plenty to do. The brain of a genius never rests.

SAME DAY, 10:00 P.M.

Well, fellow scientists, I've just attended my first band practice, and I have to say that Mrs. Bringhurst's dream of a guitar-player boyfriend for Loretta may become a reality. As I prefer participation to observation, it wasn't long before I had a guitar in my hands and Main Man was giving me my first lesson. There's a little more to playing it than I had expected, but the Rock Chompers were awed by my potential. I'm seriously considering their invitation to become an apprentice Chomper. It would be a novelty to be breaking down society rather than building it up. And can you imagine the special effects my inventions could add to the act? No, maybe the music itself is enough of a shock to the audience.

I didn't stay long because Loretta was expecting me for my first Qerbik lesson, but we didn't get much done. She taught me to say, "I love you," not for any personal reason, just because that always seems to be the first thing you learn in a foreign language.

Loretta wasn't quite sold on my band plan, but I reminded her of how happy it would make her mother.

"She doesn't care now if you're a scientist," she said. "In fact, your scientific abilities have come in handy."

We sat there on the sofa while I practiced my three-word Qerbik vocabulary, and after a while I said, "I wonder when some astronomer will discover Qerbik."

"It's discovered," Loretta said.

I sat up. "What are you talking about?" I said. "I'm sure there's no planet named Qerbik."

"Qerbik is what the Qerbikans call it," she said. "It's known here by another name."

"Loretta," I threatened, "don't make me ask."

We were alone in her living room, but she actually looked around before she whispered to me. And, fellow scientists, you would never believe the name of the planet Loretta's grandfather came from. Unfortunately, as of this writing, it's still top secret. But when I go there, scientists of the world, you'll be the first to know.